Cover image and all other images by   David Scher

Published in the United States by   Fence Books
New Library 320
University at Albany
1400 Washington Avenue
Albany, NY 12222
www.fenceportal.org

Book design by   David Scher

Fence Books are distributed by   University Press of New England
www.upne.com

and printed in Canada by   Westcan Printing Group
www.westcanpg.com

Library of Congress Cataloguing in Publication Data
        Kunin, Aaron [1973–]
        The Mandarin/ Aaron Kunin

Library of Congress Control Number: 2008920757

ISBN 1-934200-09-3
ISBN 13: 978-1-934200-09-4

FIRST EDITION

Parts of this book have appeared in *Crowd, Eleven Eleven, Fence, The Germ, No: A Journal of the Arts, Octopus, Onedit,* and *Pierogi Press.*

Fence Books are published in partnership with the New York State Writers Institute and the University at Albany.

Fence Books are made possible by generous support from the above and from the National Endowment for the Arts, the New York State Council on the Arts, and the Friends of *Fence.*

THE MANDARIN

Aaron Kunin

drawings by David Scher

ALBANY, NEW YORK

THE MANDARIN

Aaron Kunin

drawings by David Scher

CONTENTS

LIST OF ILLUSTRATIONS

Synopsis

The narrator, Willy, writes boring novels that put everyone to sleep. His sister Natasha reads one of the novels and falls asleep, and her friends try to awaken her without success: Hallamore stages elaborate spectacles for her benefit; Hallamore's sister Mercy tries to put her to work. Willy continues to write novels (the running joke is that he can write one in about an hour), although there is some question as to whether he knows what a novel is, whether he has ever read a novel: perhaps, instead of writing novels, he is producing a more potent sleep-inducing object.

The novel is set in places that no longer exist in Minneapolis—houses and apartments where one of the characters used to live, businesses and restaurants that have closed or moved elsewhere. This is why Hallamore can never get served at the Sri Lanka Curry House: because the restaurant is closed. This is why Mercy can't find any work to do at Gelpe's Bakery: because she doesn't work there anymore, because, in fact, the bakery is closed (which is also why there aren't any pastries there). This is why Willy can't open the door of his house: because it isn't his house now, it's just the house he grew up in. (This problem is complicated by the fact that he and Natasha grew up in the same house, and further complicated by the fact that, later on, they seem to have traded houses.) The characters keep returning to these non-existent places without intending to; they haunt, or are haunted by, these places.

The plot develops recursively rather than progressively, as a kind of theme-and-variations. The characters are constantly falling asleep, trying to fall asleep, waking up, or trying to wake up, so that the entire novel takes place on the border between sleep and waking. Natasha is always sleeping, so that everything that happens around her becomes a projection of what's going on inside her, in her dream.

Usually one of the characters is in a house or a room, and the others are outside trying to get in. In the first chapter, for instance, all of them seem to be lost in St. Paul, standing in front of a house

i

that they think belongs to Natasha; they can't get inside the house, and they can't confirm that it is her house, because she won't wake up. By the end of the chapter, however, Willy has asserted that they are standing in front of his own house in Minneapolis—but he still won't let them in. In the final sequence of chapters, Natasha is in her bedroom and the others are gathered outside. Willy and Hallamore enter the room, and are immediately hailed by a group of inanimate objects (T.V. set, carpet, dust-ruffle, toenail clippings, cactus). The bedroom-objects revile Hallamore and salute Willy as their long-lost brother Flavio.

The novel is written almost entirely in dialogue. There are also brief discursive passages and dialogue tags. These passages do not provide anything like exposition or immediate description; they supply only tangential information. (This procedural rule is reversed, however, in Chapters 27 and 57, which are written entirely in the voice of the first-person narrator, with dialogue given only in indirect discourse.)

As a result, actions and events tend to occur within a nimbus of uncertainty. What is certain is that the characters are speaking—and the speaker is always clearly identified—but it's never certain that their speech accurately describes the situation in which they're speaking. They may be talking about what they're actually doing in the place where they're really standing, or they may be remembering or imagining something they did or would like to be doing in another place. Any character is always capable of completely redescribing the world. For example: in Chapters 38–42, Mercy seems to be persistently phoning Willy at home. And, in a practical sense, that's what's happening, as long as the characters agree that it's happening (although these chapters leave open the possibility that the characters are all gathered in the same place to play a game in which they pretend to be talking on the phone).

Certain objects emerge as characters and are assigned voices: novel, newspaper, umbrella, telephone, T.V. set, etc. (Television is not simply a medium—part of "the media"—for T.V. *shows.* Here, it's an object, a T.V. *set,* also something that has intellect, desires, a voice; subject to its own energies and weaknesses.)

Consciousness tends to be communal rather than personal. So, for example, if Willy and Hallamore fall asleep next to each other, it's possible that Hallamore will wake up with Willy's memories and associations in his head, and that Willy, when he wakes up, will adhere to Hallamore's consciousness.

Relations between characters are predominantly fraternal-sororal. The characters don't seem to have parents (although in Chapter 8 Willy addresses Mercy and Hallamore as "Mother" and "Father"), and they don't seem to be capable of producing children. (The figure called the "biology teacher" sometimes acts as a parent for one of the characters, but this figure is more exactly equivalent to the notion of "ka" in Egyptian mythology: a more powerful version of yourself that you project in order to confuse your enemies.) Occasionally one of the characters conceives a kind of infatuation for one of the others, but this feeling is consistently one-directional: if Willy has it, Mercy and Hallamore don't have it; if Mercy has it, Willy and Hallamore don't; and so on. And if Natasha has it, no one knows about it.

Proper names are subject to similar variations. The narrator is usually called "Willy," but in Natasha's bedroom he's called "Flavio." Also, he occasionally forgets that his name isn't simply "Aaron," which is usually the name of his older brother, although in Chapter 7 "Aaron" seems to designate any person or object (such as a telephone, radio, or ventriloquist's dummy) that speaks for someone else. In Chapter 4, "Hallamore" is the name of a trucking company.

The novel does at least pretend to be an ordinary novel. It preserves the convention that the speakers are individualized characters speaking in an identifiable situation. At any moment, the characters might stop talking and start doing something. Of course, they won't, but this option is always available to them.

This book is for Amie Siegel.

I liked these people, even the most hateful among them, because they were not given the power of speech. They made themselves ridiculous in words, they struggled with words. They gazed into a distorting mirror when they spoke; they demonstrated themselves in the distortion of words, which distortion had become their alleged likeness. They made themselves vulnerable when they courted understanding; they accused one another so unsuccessfully that insult sounded like praise and praise like insult.

Elias Canetti, *The Torch in My Ear*

1. Dream on this a little more

As usual, everything Hallamore said was shit.

"The form is softness," said Hallamore, "as though one were to take softness and make of it a hard form, as though one were to hold softness in the hand and say, 'Behold! Softness, you are changed! You are our champion, softness, and this is a supple, flowing world!' The form is softness, but it is a hard softness. Like the wind."

"What you say means nothing," said Mercy. "What you say is nothing but the purest shit. And there's softness for you: shit. Yeah, that's the only thing that's soft these days. And you were wrong, you were wrong with what you said about the wind: these days the wind is hard, not soft. These days things stand pretty much as they did a long time ago, when a gust of wind was like a piece of furniture that you could put your hat and coat on. That's true, you could hang your hat on the wind, and when you opened your mouth it was like drowning: the wind knocked the wind out of you."

"Lost in St. Paul again," I said. "Not to mention the inside of my mouth, which is cut up from eating a big piece of chocolate. I have to collect these pieces of food (candies, nuts, lumps of sugar) for my biology teacher, because he is supposed to be so holy and respectable that he can manufacture gods and angels out of them in his tubby little belly. The gods and angels are supposed to set me free—from what, I don't know."

And Natasha, who was asleep, said nothing.

There we all were; I remember everything perfectly. Mercy and Hallamore, Natasha and I, my ratty winter coat, the back of Hallamore's head, Mercy's ugly white car, the darkened houses of the city gathered in around us, the windows of the houses glowing faintly with the light that comes from television sets, this light reflected in the ice on the street, the sidewalk, and so on.

"I had said, 'Let's take five,'" said Mercy, "and I had a cup of coffee and an apple, and she fell asleep; I found her on the sofa, asleep. In her hand she had a bunch of papers that had

Concupiscence, a novel written on them."

"Now Natasha isn't lazy," I said. "Really I'm the lazy one. Although I prefer the word 'sedentary.' In bed at night I get so frustrated with my pillow that I sometimes throw it across the room because it keeps me awake, it is oppressively soft. Then I whisper into the mattress that my bed is a gloomy fortress, and the bedsprings send back an echo, as though a person (imprisoned in the mattress) were praying to be released. I imagine sinking into the mattress . . . it would be punishing, it would be like getting beat up. The mattress itself is veined with things that hurt you when you take a breath from the thick air that rises from it and hurt you again when you exhale into it, as though with each breath from the mattress a swarm of insects came in at your nostrils and built a nest in your chest. I wake up sneezing, retrieve the pillow from across the room—the pillowcase smells musty—turn over on my back. An early-morning bird cries out outside my window at irregular intervals. A devil whispers in my ear, 'There is no variety, there is no vicissitude, there is no good, no delight, no mixture of pleasure and pain'; someone is shoveling the sidewalk. I'm out of bed; I knuckle the windowpane and the early-morning bird takes off, still crying out; the sun is a fist; the sun showers light that feels like blows to the head. I haven't slept. Instead I have written a novel in pencil on the wall: *Belligerence, a novel.*"

"When Shakespeare says that life is a dream," said Hallamore, "he seems to mean that it's a big hoax. But when King talks about the dream of his life, he means something we should demand and be angry about when it doesn't happen. These two ideas can be combined:

> I have had a dream past the wit of man to say what
> dream it was. I have had a dream that my four little
> children will one day live in a nation where they will
> be judged not by the color of their skin but by the
> content of their character. I will get Peter Quince
> to write a ballad of this dream. It shall be called
> 'Bottom's Dream,' because it hath no bottom . . .

6

"I believe that we should be made to suffer for actions committed in dreams: in our own dreams and when we appear to others in dreams. And when I say that the form is softness, I mean that you should take my play in the softest possible sense."

"Letter A, no one wants to hear about your play," said Mercy. "And B, the only softness I see here is your own softness of the brain. You can't just go around flashing softness. C, there is a stench in the nostrils of St. Peter, who watches over us and punishes us. The finest act, the most generous act we can concoct, he hates. St. Peter thinks you should be caned for the line you drew on your arm in magic marker when you were in the third grade. St. Peter wants to hurl you into the brownest cesspool at the bottom of the hottest hell for making a big deal out of it when someone mispronounces your name. St. Peter wants to crush you beneath his thumb for disturbing the pigeons when you open the window. He wants to punch you in the nose for swearing at a dog, for tipping your waiter more than you can afford, for making your friends uncomfortable with the intensity of your friendship. Of course he holds your dreams against you! Of course he holds it against you that you visit others in dreams and haunt their sleep with your image! And for that, St. Peter would like to have you screwed into a brick wall, because that's what I would like, for everything you've ever done, for not believing in Santa Claus, anything, Hallamore, hypocrite, angel-eyes, darling!"

"I want to thank you for getting me out of the restaurant," I said. "That was the restaurant where they play Dave Brubeck's 'Take Five' forever; I would never have eaten there if I had known it was that restaurant. The chair they put me in was a Mies van der Rohe chair, and even the chair was playing Dave Brubeck's 'Take Five,' which begins with a robust fart and ends with a wet kiss. I said, 'I'll have this-and-that in a glass,' and they said, 'Fart.' I said, 'I'll have such-and-such on a plate,' and they said, 'Kiss.' I said, 'Could I have the check, please?' and they said, 'Fart,' and I wrote another novel, *The Discovery of Pockets, a novel,* on the placemat. It's a good thing you abducted me from the restaurant, that's for sure; did you notice, on the way out, how the revolving door went fart, kiss, fart, kiss, fart, kiss? Generally I agree with you, Mercy, only I never say so. When I say there is a hell in the lives of fools I mean that St. Peter punishes us for a lot of things, but mostly he punishes us for our stupidity. That is why, Hallamore, so many of the dead end up in hell. Because they are very stupid. Just ask the dead to write a simple sentence for you, something easy, such as WHAT DOES TINA DO ON SUNDAY MORNING? And they don't know, it comes out all garbled, like WHAT DOSE TOM DOE ON SUNDAY MORNING? That's why I say, no civil rights for the dead."

"I want to ask a question," said Hallamore. "Would there be love if there were no poets? I'm serious, would love exist if there were no word for it?"

"Ridiculous," I said.

"Go away," said Mercy.

"But," said Hallamore, "the act of writing is an act of love; the act of love is a literary act; and when I say that I am in love, that is an interpretation, and interpretation is the domain of literary criticism (and theology!). And that is why I say that all her brutishness, all her hardness, her aggressiveness, her provocativeness, her belligerence—is love. Suddenly she becomes a philosophical figure, an allegorical figure—and her name, in fact, is Mercy. Her name leads us to expect that she will be forgiving. Her name promises absolution, and she breaks that promise every time you say her name and she turns toward you. She promised forgiveness, and you should demand the fulfillment of that promise and be angry at its retraction, but don't get angry at me, because she's the one who promised, not me."

"How will it be shown, though?" I said. "Through what channel will her clemency be broadcast?"

"Easy," said Hallamore. "CNN! Yes, it would be so remarkable to hear a kind word from my sister that it would actually be reported on CNN. It is a gracious world; it is a merciful world; it is a soft world; and CNN is all of these. And she is Mercy. She locks her hands together and draws them slowly down, cracking her knuckles like Robert Mitchum."

"What you see is all there is," said Mercy. "Natasha is asleep:

there is the world's grace. What you see is all there is: the door to her house is locked. I disdain you, Hallamore: there is the world's mercy. What you see is all there is: the garden is buried in snow. Natasha's cat, Thisbe, rolls in the grass and scrapes the snow off her back: there is all the softness in the world. There is no way in; what you see is all there is—my hardness? I know I'm supposed to be Mercy, but shit! I'm saying something here. I'm cold, wet, hungry, and tired, and wind is cutting me like a knife, it seems, from all sides. I've come all the way from the other end of the city to deliver Natasha, my friend, to her home."

"I have written a play for Natasha," said Hallamore.

"I'm Natasha's brother," I said. "All of us are in St. Paul."

"Here we are in St. Paul," said Mercy, "on the sidewalk in front of Natasha's house. It's late. There are no masks, the only illusion is illusion, nothing is shadow. Because if you really think about the nature of the world, you will conclude that there is no color in it, and no savor, and no perfume, and no consistency, and it is as silent as mud. Because it's made of one material, and it's not water, fire, or air—as though this dirty world, this earth, could be made of anything but earth! As though the world could be anything but buried beneath earth, as though, where we are, underground, we could be free (as though sticking a flag in something could set it free, as though the moon were free). And that is my frustration, and that is our frustration, and as for you," turning to me, "why don't YOU speak up, YOU get us into Natasha's house, YOU haven't said anything this whole time! You have your finger over your lips whenever I see you; I guess you must be the god of silence."

"The world is buried to me," I said. "I look at the sky; the sky is buried. I've made some mistakes: okay. When we were on Excelsior and I bit Mercy's arm and forced her to run a red light, and she wanted to know the way home, and I didn't know what street it was on, and I don't know what I said, but it was wrong . . . This isn't Natasha's house after all. This isn't even St. Paul. This is Minneapolis, and this is my house. Look at this cat rolling in the grass: it's Thatbe, the spite cat. You know, when Natasha kicked me out of her house, I got a cat, and out of spite (because I think Thisbe

9

is a terrible name for a cat) I called it Thatbe. And I'm not going to let you in, if that's what you are thinking. I'm about to write a novel, here, on the sidewalk: *Piss and Bellow, Kick and Wiggle,* a novel. It was nice of you to get me out of the restaurant and everything. But really nothing we do can help Natasha, because it appears that she read one of my novels, which you should never do, because anyone who reads one of my novels falls asleep and never wakes up. *Concupiscence, a novel:* sure, I wrote that. It's terrible living in Minneapolis and hating the novel as much as I do—you start to think about it and it keeps you awake until you're the only person left awake in the city. I even wrote to the manufacturer of sleeping pills for some sleeping pills, but apparently everyone at the factory was asleep."

2. There are neither paragraphs nor regulations!

"There are certain unwritten rules for living in the city," said Mercy.

"You must never hold or brush against the handrails when you are on the stairs," I said. "The handrails are coated with dried piss. Why is it there? How did it get there?"

"The first thing you must do," said Hallamore, "when you think you are going crazy, is to look in the mirror."

"I try to stay away from lunatics," said Mercy, "because I don't want to be the one who made them that way."

"Don't bother to count your socks," I said, "since it will only make you sad."

"You spend money just doing nothing," said Hallamore. "You were sitting in the same chair all day, only listening to the radio or reading, and somewhere in there you bought a pack of gum. That's a dollar seventy-five in one sitting."

"Jim ate a pound of arsenic," said Mercy. "Anyone who eats a pound of arsenic dies within twenty-four hours."

"You can drown in a bucket," said Hallamore, "or in the kitchen sink, or in a well, or at the bottom of a lake. You're drowning, Willy: get your head out of the water!"

"My throat is a little sore," I said. "Or, as they say in St. Paul: my voice went on vacation."

"All of us must be Christ," said Hallamore.

"Eskimos have only one word for snow," said Mercy.

"The word in Eskimo for snow," said Hallamore, "is the same as the word in Eskimo for spitballs."

"I am taller than my brother," said Mercy. "I like to hang my pictures high."

"I know that I am of average height," said Hallamore, "because the graffiti over the urinal is at my eye-level."

"Sometimes," I said, "nature furnishes us with symbols so obvious that it becomes our moral obligation to ignore them."

"The history of the human race," said Mercy, "is the history of a handful of misplaced commas, quotation marks, apostrophes, and decimal points."

"There are brackets in the world," said Hallamore. "We live in parenthesis, the blink of an eye, the corner of a mouth."

"Another long day of turning and turning off one another," I said, "in a crowded room. Excuse me!—Oh, hello!—Sorry!—Here I am again!—Oh, dear!"

"And that window in which," said Hallamore, "whenever you go by it, you find a woman taking off her shirt, or her sweater, or something: her arms above her head, her breasts dangling, her elbows out."

"You say things that are false and strange," said Mercy. "You should be condemned in the name of letters and science. Elbows out, they don't dangle, they stretch up!"

"There's a kind of power in silence," I said. "The greatest power is not speaking."

"There's a ton of power in not speaking," said Mercy. "Biting your tongue to keep from talking is powerful. But there's more power in not laughing."

"The best power is not writing," I said.

"The best power is to suppress or swallow a joke," said Mercy.

"In a way," said Hallamore, "we're all right."

"I hate anyone who looks the least bit like me," said Mercy, "anyone whose voice is like my voice, anyone who agrees with me, especially on subjects such as art, books, and music."

"I'm sorry for everything," I said. "I'm sorry for things that are not my fault."

"But you don't," said Hallamore, "you can't possibly understand. None of you understands! All this—I did all this because of my sister. And she didn't even show up!"

"Before I can understand something," said Mercy, "I have to classify it. A fact by itself doesn't mean anything."

"There are no flowers in the clouds," I said.

"Even fools have hell," said Mercy.

"I can't tell you," I said, "how grateful I am for this opportunity to say a few words about dust."

"Without our burnt offerings," said Mercy, "St. Peter would have to eat in the kitchen."

"St. Peter must love abandoned restaurants, because he made so many of them," said Hallamore.

"He must love pockets," said Mercy, "because he put four of them on this pair of pants."

"The world we inhabit is a wreck of paradise," said Hallamore. "Proving that the world was created."

"Proof is no substitute for the act of creation," said Mercy.

"Poetry is a kind of dumping ground," said Hallamore.

"Society is a lie," I said.

"Poetry must be elitist," said Hallamore.

"There is a cost," I said.

"It is possible," said Hallamore, "to squeeze blood out of this turnip."

"The earth is female," said Mercy. "The sky is male."

"The wind is male," said Hallamore. "The snow is female."

"The vine is female," said Mercy. "The elm is male."

"The circle is male," said Hallamore. "The triangle is female."

"The female curve," said Mercy. "The rigid male line."

"The gods of Minneapolis are male," said Hallamore. "The gods of St. Paul are goddesses."

"Hats are female; hat racks are male," said Mercy. "Every time you hang your hat on the rack, there is a subtext of fucking."

"Or if you put the hat on your head," said Hallamore.

"Is a man's hat just as female as a woman's hat is?" I said.

"Or if you put one hat on top of another," said Mercy.

"Or a circle in another circle," I said.

"We all practice dialectic," said Mercy. "A dog learns to come when her name is called, and not when someone turns on the radio—she practices dialectic. You could compare this building to a flea—that, too, would be dialectic."

"We are all shadowboxing," I said. "We all shadowbox, but no two people shadowbox in quite the same way. I hide my face behind my fists and throw in the towel; Hallamore here feints to the right;

Mercy leads with her left and wipes her nose with her right, almost stumbling over Natasha, who doesn't shadowbox."

"We are all comedians," said Hallamore. "Every comedian is wrong about something. There's a place for those of us who don't belong."

Even fools have hell.

3. The little Minneapolis theater of the world

Then Mercy began her complaint: "These days we break ourselves against the world like an uncertain continuous line being drawn on the sidewalk in chalk."

And Hallamore began his complaint: "These days the whale is a symbol for baseball."

And I, too, complained: "These days souls ascend to heaven only when their machinery is perfect."

And the wind complained: "These days softness means hating everything that isn't soft."

And the house complained: "These days the point is not to build a better mousetrap, but to get the official mouse monopoly."

And the sky complained: "These days the marquis tries to find his own way out, but he wanders into a broom closet, and no one hears from him for many years."

And the sidewalk complained: "These days Lady Macbeth hides her hands behind her back, crossing her fingers."

And Thatbe, the spite cat, complained: "These days you have to take a multiple-choice test in a magazine just to find out if you're a man or a woman."

"How can you be a whale and be baseball at the same time?" Mercy wanted to know.

"Baseball pervades the whale," said Hallamore. "The limits of the whale are also its limits."

"These days," I complained, "no one understands the 'silly question, silly answer' principle."

"These days no one shows mercy except on CNN," said Hallamore.

"A curse on you for saying that stupid thing," said Mercy. "Ladies and gentlemen, he's as dumb as we thought!"

"Hallamore is the sort of person who would make a terrible comedian," complained Thatbe, the spite cat. "Naturally he's a comedian."

"Hey Hallamore, you old softie," said the sidewalk, "did you unleash your entire wit on this poor woman's head? Oh, thou art a most unscrupulous comedian!"

"Your name," complained Mercy. "Like your sex, it's something just dropped in your lap. You could always try changing it, but then you might make it worse."

"These days they put you in jail for keeping sheep," complained the wind.

"These days they put you in jail for chewing gum," complained the house.

"If your house is the wrong color," the sky complained, "they put you in jail."

"For playing hopscotch," the sidewalk complained, "they put you in jail."

"Playing hopscotch with malicious intent," my cat said spitefully.

And I also complained: "These days most speech is incoherent. You might as well bang on a pot—it's just as meaningless. In fact, all incoherent people do wear pots around their necks so that they can drown out anything sensible by banging on their pots with wooden spoons. The din is unbearable."

"These days there are orgies everywhere," said Hallamore. "Even the Bible contains orgies these days."

"This man claims that the Bible contains orgies," complained the sidewalk.

"The Bible contains no orgies," said Thatbe, with spite. "The Bible can't contain orgies, according to Axel Olrik's laws of oral literature. Second law, no more than two characters to a scene."

And the sky complained: "These days a plate with an apple on it is good luck."

And Thatbe complained: "These days fish fingers are also good luck."

And the sidewalk complained: "These days a table that isn't there is more of a table than the table right in front of you. It doesn't matter how much you crack your elbows on the table."

And the house complained: "These days a dead whale is more of a whale than a living one."

And the earth complained: "These days baseball is more of a whale than most whales."

"These days," complained Mercy, "the Renaissance begins on page twenty-eight of the Michelin guide to Italy."

"These days," complained Hallamore, "they give medals to soldiers for drinking the right kind of root beer. Why, just the other day, I opened the mailbox, and someone had sent me a medal: for drinking the right kind of root beer."

I agreed. "All poets are failed soldiers, Hallamore."

"People you can't convert," said Mercy. "Or animals you can't convert. Those taped messages: 'You are no good; you will never make it.' It's no use saying: 'Yes, I can; I am good!' You have to break the circle; you have to stop the tape."

"Against logic," complained the house. "Because it is on a wild goose chase."

"Against grammar," complained the sky. "Because it is uncorrupted, and no one can really touch it."

"Against rhetoric," complained the wind. "Because things that are sweet should be avoided."

"Against arithmetic," complained the earth. "Because it is an invention of the nineteenth century."

"Against geometry," complained the sidewalk. "Because it runs faster."

"Against music," complained Thatbe, the spite cat. "Because I do not appreciate it."

"Against astronomy," complained the sky. "Because we should rely on what we see, not on stories people tell."

"Against the mathematicians," I complained. "Because of their noses, because of the pants they wear. Because they want pastries, because the mathematician who has the most pastries has the most power, because the most powerful mathematician, Brenda, can kill all her enemies in one blow. Because she doesn't want them to have any pastries."

"Against the poets," complained Mercy. "Because of their hands, because of the pockets in which they stick them. Because you are either a friend of Socrates or an enemy of Socrates. Because all poets are enemies of Socrates. Because they killed Socrates, because they wanted to kill Descartes, because they killed King. Because Descartes, too, had a dream. Because Descartes cut the throat of poetry, because, when I think, I am René Descartes, because, when I sleep, I am a poet. Because the essence of being a poet is sleeping and screwing around."

"Against the comedians," complained Hallamore. "Because of their lips, because of the insides of their mouths. Because traces of what you eat remain in your mouth, dispersed across your mouth in crevices between the teeth. Because smells of food linger in rooms, even when no one has eaten there, because you can smell it in the furniture, the chairs and pillows, when you sink into them, because not all of what you eat goes into you, but remains in pieces on the table and the plate and in the air. Because food remains in the body as well, because essentially no transformation has taken place between what you put in and what comes out, because food enters the body with no change in its composition, remaining essentially what it was, whereas a word passes through many mouths and is never dirty."

And Natasha, who was asleep, did not complain.

4. Morbid sleep

"I've written another novel," I said. "I don't know what effect this one will have on my readers, but it made me rather hungry."

"What's this one about?" said Mercy.

"No one has ever asked me that before," I said. "The reviews were terrible. They all complained about its sleep-inducing quality."

"Most reviews are written in sleep anyway," said Mercy.

"I don't see how a sleeping person could write a book review," said Hallamore. He always said his name was Hallamore, Peter Hallamore, Bernard Peter Hallamore, or something like that. But really it wasn't anything like Hallamore. I don't know where he got that name. I believe he read it off the side of a truck.

"The narcotic effect of your novels is singular, and needs to be studied," said Mercy. "Does it take effect the moment you open the book? Or does a feeling of drowsiness gradually come over you as you read it, until you finally drop off at the bottom of the last page? Or does the volume give off a sleeping agent that affects anyone who gets close enough?"

"Even talking about it could be risky," said Hallamore.

"The first person I ever put to sleep, with a novel, was Eric Liu," I said. "Eric Liu, a friend of my sister's, asked to hear part of the novel I was working on, so I read a few pages to him, just to give him an idea of what it was like; once, while I was reading, I looked up, and he had fallen asleep with his chin resting on his hand. I looked down and continued reading. . . . The pauses in my reading were filled with his quiet, thoughtful snores."

"Is reading it what makes you fall asleep?" said Mercy. "Does it have anything to do with the paper you're using? The ink?"

"I once read a novel that made me want to kill myself," said Hallamore. "But it didn't have that effect on everyone who read it."

5. (Herself) in collusion

"You're probably wondering," said Mercy, "where I was born."

"Well, no," I said.

"Probably it would interest you to know where I work."

"No."

"I guess you must be dying to know that I work in a place called Gelpe's Old World Bakery."

"If you say so."

"You can scarcely contain your curiosity about the girl I work with, whose name is Leah Gelpe."

"Well, no, not really."

"In the morning, where I work, the floor is cold and the air smells of sour milk. Leah Gelpe, my boss, is vomiting into the toilet. What a night I had last night. There was a mosquito in bed with me, whispering in my ear and giving me horrid dreams, and I must have been biting my lip all night, because part of it is swollen and I can hardly speak."

"Are you still talking out there?" said Leah Gelpe. "Why don't you do something with your life; get a job; make a baguette, a croissant, or a petit-four?"

"Leah Gelpe," said Mercy, "like Don Quixote, read the *chansons de geste* and wanted to be like Roland, so she spent the rest of her life vomiting into the toilet and mooning over dry biscuits and petits-fours. Get this: she wants me to work on my hands and knees because I'm taller than she is. Don't you like tall women, Leah Gelpe?

"I crouch at her feet. Is there nothing I can do to please your taste, my own cruel, serene, impenetrable, but tender and exquisite, employer?"

"Hey, guys, did I miss anything?" said Hallamore.

"I see that Hallamore has decided to put in an appearance," said Mercy. "There he stands, grinning sheepishly, clutching his vanilla milkshake—only two hours late."

"I want to enter this store," said Hallamore. "I enter: a warm breeze salutes me, animated by particles of flour and the delightful smell of yeast. It is unbearably pleasant to think about the forbidden pastries in their display cases; this thought, combined with the actual milkshake which I can still taste at the end of my straw, completely destroys me."

"Forbidden by whom?" I said.

"Forbidden by my biology teacher," said Hallamore. "And one mustn't disobey one's biology teacher, must one?"

"Cowlick," said Leah Gelpe, "cauliflower, ape! Corn-fed Hallamore, inbred Hallamore, trick-knee'd, knock-knee'd, hackneyed Hallamore; towheaded, dough-headed, bowlegged— Hallamore, you are crow's feet to me; you are flies in my soup to me; why should my time with you be poisoned with such thoughts?"

"I'm looking for a meringue to worship," said Hallamore. "If I ate one of your meringues, then I would possess a godlike knowledge."

"When I first saw Leah Gelpe whipping a meringue, I thought she was crazy," said Mercy. "And when I saw bagels being put in boiling water, I was horrified. 'What are they doing to the bagels,' etc. Come down here, Willy."

"Ow," I said.

"Early in the morning, this floor is carpeted with strudel dough," said Mercy. "You put your arms in it and roll it out, and you are in flour up to your elbows; you become like a big butter-and-egg man in your labor."

"Out of all the things that are possible," I said, "this is the one that's apparent to you." Meanwhile I wrote another novel in the steam on the glass, *Sick of Irony, a novel.*

"This is our display case," said Mercy. "See? It unlocks when you put a key in it, just like an empty cabinet that you might have at home. To the left you will find other locked cabinets that work in the same way. Now, on the countertop—look where I'm pointing— here, this is our glass bell which I bet you could just fit under."

"Look, Hallamore," said Leah Gelpe, "are you going to buy something, or what?"

"Sure I will buy something," said Hallamore. "I'll buy—this."

"Leave me alone, then," said Leah Gelpe.

"No, wait," said Hallamore, "I can't make up my mind."

"Do you want to buy some day-old bread," said Mercy, "at half-price?"

"Yeah, sure," said Hallamore.

"We're out of day-old bread," said Leah Gelpe. "Why don't you come back when you want to buy something real."

"I do want to buy something," said Hallamore. "Here, look, I'll take—one of these." A pack of gum.

"A pack of gum!" said Leah Gelpe. "You have got to be kidding! We don't even sell that; you brought that in here; I'm not going to sell that to you. Where did you—hey, you, put down that pastry bag, what are you supposed to be, some kind of guerilla novelist?" So I had to leave my work in progress, *The Busman's Holiday, a novel,* in icing on yellow cake, in a state of incompletion.

"Yellow cake is just what I want," said Hallamore.

"That is a salt cake," said Mercy. "My remedial reading students have made a salt cake to demonstrate the benefits of reading. The idea is that children who can't read will have to eat cakes made with salt for the rest of their lives because they might choose the wrong package and put salt in the batter if they couldn't tell the word SALT apart from the word SUGAR."

"Or if they couldn't taste the sweetness of the sugar," I said.

"Advances in reading have made it impossible for anyone to eat this cake," said Mercy. "We exhibit this cake as a monument to the rewards of reading."

"I'm sorry I ruined your cake," I said.

6. Design for living

"Something happens to my voice," I said, "when I try to order food in a restaurant. Suddenly it's very faint . . . I can hardly make a sound. I point to what I want on the menu, and the waiter still doesn't understand and asks me to say it again. I'm shouting and he still can't hear it (to me it sounds as though I'm shouting). My voice has a harsh sound to it. . . . It sounds like a little girl trying to sound like a certain kind of middle-aged man, a pompous one who has an exaggerated idea of his importance. This man doesn't even exist; nonetheless there's something in my voice that's very close to that. It doesn't make me sound middle-aged, it makes me sound confused and ashamed. Eventually I become ashamed of the food I'm asking for after trying to give its name several times. The name sounds peculiar to me: I forget how to pronounce it; the way I'm pronouncing it sounds wrong; maybe I'm saying another word without realizing. I start to wish that I had tried to order something else; I think that something else on the menu might not have given me so much trouble. This is something I have to consider when I look at a menu: what name on the menu will I be able to say most clearly?"

"You can see him struggle, even now, to complete a sentence," said Hallamore. "You can tell that he has only one word in his head, that he is reluctant to use it; he knows it isn't right, but pushes ahead anyway, parting his lips to begin saying the nauseating word in an effort to prolong a condition of—what shall I call it?—facility, he thinks. But it isn't that; that is what he does not have; that was closed to him before he started talking."

"Why did I start talking?" I said. "Only so that there would be something to say, something to shift the burden of the conversation ('burden of the conversation'—nauseating phrase). Maybe if I put some words together, I thought, if I put some words together, maybe I can talk myself out of it."

"He says one word, then another," said Mercy. "The words do not cling; they do not make a sentence. It becomes an effort

"Can you pick me up after work?"
"Well, my biology teacher told me not to."

to speak to him, so that we have to consider what we are going to
say before we can bring ourselves to say it, which somehow makes
what we say messier and more confused, less guarded rather than
more so. And this is also liberating, it is also liberating when he
misunderstands what we are trying to say, which pleases us; it is a
positive pleasure to misunderstand for a change. We feel, in his
presence, as though someone else is speaking for us, as though, by
refusing to talk, he has made himself responsible for everything we
say. It's like trying on a suit that doesn't fit: suddenly you arrive at a
new understanding of your shape and size."

"He pauses," said Hallamore, "touching his lips to stop himself
from talking, to push a button, turn them off. Then he draws his
hand across his mouth as though cleaning himself like a cat, to
wipe away the residue of his speech, and also to see if there's any
talk left there, around his lips—to make sure that they aren't still
talking."

"Better check again," said Mercy.

"And also to calm the lips after their ordeal," said Hallamore,
"caressing them, congratulating them for what they have done,
rewarding the mouth for speech, pointing to the lips to show where
the talking came from, taking credit for speech without speaking.
And finally rubbing them: to recharge them."

"I can't talk," I said. "It becomes an effort to speak, which
makes what I say effortless; I put so much care into what I say that
it becomes careless, as though I had cared so much about what
I was going to say that I couldn't care any more, as though, in
putting all my care into choosing the words, I had nothing left to
put in, and could only spit them out in an unpunctuated jumble.
Possessed by a desire to cry out, to burst into song, I remember that
such an outburst is usually accompanied by a little pain; I make a
tentative sound, confirming that this pain exists, is always there,
latent, waiting to be expressed in a cry that is its cause as well as its
language. (The memory, too, is tentative. Is it also painful?)"

"He forces it out of his mouth," said Hallamore, "for no other
reason than to get it out of his mouth, to prove that he can really
do it. Once out of his mouth it is no less burdensome than when

it was in his mouth. The word comes out, and he wants to hide it, to attribute it to someone else. He speaks quickly—to get it over with."

"I force myself out of the house," I said, "for no other reason than to get myself out of the house, to prove that I can still do it. Once out of the house I spend the rest of the day looking at reproductions of the objects I left back at my house, coming up with the same ideas, digesting the same food—maybe if I ate another kind of food, if someone else prepared my food, if I went out of the house to eat it, then maybe I would have different ideas."

"More superstition!" said Hallamore. "Everything you know about your body, about disease, about sex and food, is nothing but prejudice and superstition. What you actually put in your body makes no difference; your body would produce the same thing out of any materials."

"My body is responding to something in my mind," I said. "If I could stop having these thoughts, maybe I could stop eating this food, then possibly I could rest."

"I force everything out of my mouth," said Leah Gelpe. "I force myself to expel everything that enters me, everything I take in: the walls of my stomach shiver and lift; acid rises in my throat, searing my vocal cords ('searing' them—nauseating phrase), and my stomach's contents spill out, first gray, then gold, then orange, because I started by putting in something bright orange so that I would know, when it stopped coming out orange, that it was finished. Once out of my mouth this reflux seems more hateful than when I kept it inside—then, at least, it was hidden; now the sight makes me gag, but I have nothing left to give but my own innards, my own bile, the lining of my stomach. I void myself, I spit myself out; I want to draw a circle around me and force myself out of the circle. I keep flushing the toilet—is it possible that there is no emotion in all this noise?—and it won't go down; it comes back hissing, somewhat diluted, monochromatic. Maybe this wasn't what I wanted in the beginning, but I can't remember and it all seems very unimportant now."

"What is my life?" said Mercy. "Waking and sleeping; talking, mouths biting air; eating and digesting and repeating . . . consuming the same materials to nourish the same thoughts, the same words. A lifetime of needless repetitions."

"A lifetime of needless repetitions," said Leah Gelpe. "And here I call foul—'call foul,' foul, nauseating phrase ('nauseating phrase,' nauseating phrase); the taste is constantly in your mouth. You can't get away from eating and drinking and evacuating (pissing and shitting). Never digestion. Never nourishment."

"Eating is repeating," said Mercy. "My lips part and fuse, rebound and draw back, trying to form the same words, the same phrase, with each bite: I am eating the dead . . . I am eating the dead . . . until I am filled with death."

"Because I love animals," I said, "I eat only vegetables."

"Superstition!" said Hallamore. "Isn't it better for those who love animals to consume them, so that those who hate them can abstain?"

"I realize now that I'm only a collection of superstitions," I said. "Dead thoughts, dead ideas. An idea that's dead leaves a disturbance in the mind, like the disturbance in the air that a person creates exiting a room. A body goes out of a room: other bodies remain in the room, breathing in its wind, and you're left with a feeling that that body is still standing there. 'It was here; I saw it and touched it. How can I believe that it's no longer here?'"

"Destruction makes an appearance," said Mercy. "Or is it only the appearance of destruction? The apparition of an idea or a building that has been destroyed? What will happen to the people who lived in this building?"

"I promise you new ideas and a new home!" said Hallamore. "A promise that I have already broken."

"I promise you a new life!" I said. "A promise that I have no intention of keeping."

"I promise you a new language!" said Mercy. "A promise that will probably mean something quite different in my new language."

"I made a promise with my mouth," I said. "My hands broke it."

7. The destruction of appearances

"What's a thought?" said Leah Gelpe, tearing the front of her coat. "An event in the mind? (Can a thought take place only in the mind? But where is the mind?) And what about ideas? Is an idea like a mental or physical object? A thought cut out of the mind? A thought crystallized—idealized—so that you can hand it to someone? A gift, such as a friend gives to a friend? Oh thoughts and ideas, why do you let me sound like a moron? Why do you give me leave to live in the moron's mouth and sleep in the moron's bed where I have to bear the embraces of the moron? Why must I put my head on the moron's pillow, consult with him and play hide-and-go-seek with him?"

"I understand what you're trying to say," said Mercy, raising her hand in a kind of salute.

"Will you say it for me then?" said Leah Gelpe, putting her hands in her pockets and taking them out again. "Will you talk to me, and put words in my mouth, and sit with me in my mouth, and in my ear, and tell me what to say?"

"We all use puppets," said Hallamore, absently arranging his hair in a way that made him look inhuman. "We call them Aarons, because Aaron was Moses's puppet in ancient myth. I am the Aaron of Leah Gelpe: I speak for her to the people."

"We all use spokespersons," said Mercy, backing into a wall.

"We are all mouthpieces," said Hallamore, without opening his mouth.

"You are all bullshit artists," said Leah Gelpe, rolling up her sleeves, "and brilliant young things pontificating."

"We all have an Aaron," said Mercy, ripping pages out of a book and scattering them on the floor. "I am the Aaron of Hallamore, because no one else will believe him or listen to his voice."

"I feel ridiculous in this sweater," said Hallamore, and started to pull it over his head.

"I am the Aaron of Natasha," I said. "Is that right?"

"Judy! Judy! Where is Judy!" said Hallamore.

"Here I am, Mr. Punch," said Mercy. "Give me a raisin cookie?"

"Coffee?" said Leah Gelpe.

"Two coffees," said Mercy.

"A coffee and an egg," said Hallamore.

"Another coffee," said Mercy.

"You guys are like the Egyptian parliament!" said Leah Gelpe.

8. Her refusal to serve any customer

"I will not serve," said Leah Gelpe. "I will not serve you. It is not my pleasure to serve you. Is this your home? Am I your servant? Your personal chef? No!"

"The customer also serves," said Hallamore, "who only stands and waits."

"I am standing and waiting to serve you," I said. "It is my pleasure to serve you."

"The masochist is always ready to serve," said Mercy. "Oh Justine, you must wear a tighter corset, and long white gloves trimmed with fur and studded with shiny silver buttons that pinch. Here, let me button them for you (can't you do anything right?). Justine, pick up those cinders out of the grate, but be sure not to soil your long white gloves with ash."

"Justine, where's my breakfast?" said Hallamore. "Hurry up with the toast, but don't bring it too close to the fire, or it will burn. And I hope for your sake you are not going to tear it with the toasting-fork."

"Why would they call their child Justine?" said Leah Gelpe. "Life for him can only be a series of ever more constricting corsets."

"I have trouble recognizing my name when I hear it," I said. "It sounds as though it must refer to someone else, and then it seems to be changing all the time."

"Maybe he's one of the people in this room who have no first name," said Mercy. "Eh, Mr. Hallamore?"

"Mercy," said Leah Gelpe, "isn't your name also Hallamore?"

"False! Mine is Carbonell," said Mercy. "My brother and I chose different names so that no one would know what name we share."

"Mother! Father!" I said. "I've made a bed for you that you can die in! Look what I've made!"

9. A bed made of newspaper

"The newspaper is in the bed," I said. "The bed is dying . . ."

"It's not a dying-bed, it's a life-producing bed," said Hallamore. "It has everything you'll need for the afterlife, and it has everything you'll need in case you want to make a bed in the afterlife so that you can die in it and move on into the life after that."

"This bed will live forever," I said. "Anyone who sleeps in this bed will live forever."

"In this bed you have made something that will never die," said Hallamore. "But it's much more difficult to make a bed that will die . . ."

"My bed dies every night and returns to life in the morning," I said. "And I live and die with my bed . . ."

"That bed has good stuff in it," said Mercy. "I always suspected that your talent was for bed-making, since you're so good at making things that put everyone to sleep."

"Whatever a bed is made with, I don't have it," said Hallamore. "My bed is hard as a board."

"That's because you're using a board," I said.

"I have an idea for a bed," said Hallamore. "I mean, an idea for something to do in bed. Move over, let me get into bed with you, and I'll tell it to you."

"A bed isn't made with ideas," I said. "It's made with the hands."

"What if you made a bed with ideas (instead of whatever a bed is really made of)?" said Hallamore. "What if you made a bed out of the very idea of softness? Would that make it especially comfy, or would it just fall apart, not hold its shape? What if you made it with sleep itself? Would you be able to fall asleep in a bed that someone had put together unconsciously?"

"A bed isn't made with softness, it's made with foam," I said. "A bed isn't made with sleep, it's made with feathers and wood."

"Willy, I want to fall asleep in your bed," said Hallamore. "I want to wear your clothes, I want to eat the food out of your mouth . . ."

"For some people, just getting you into their apartment is enough," I said. "For some people, just getting into bed is enough. Or just undressing."

"If Willy and Hallamore fall asleep next to each other," said Mercy, "if they wake up in the same bed, and they start to rebuild the separate machineries they use to apprehend the world, they might not be able to tell which consciousness was theirs."

"If you fall asleep next to me, you might wake up with my ideas in your head," said Hallamore. "But you wouldn't know they were my ideas."

"If you fall asleep in my bed, it might give you a different perspective," I said. "It might give you new ideas. Because when you wake up, you adhere to the ideas close to you, the knowledge in the immediate vicinity."

"If you fall asleep next to me, it might give you a more accurate knowledge than you can endure," said Hallamore. "You might not sleep well. You might never sleep again."

"I'm giving up sleep," I said. "But I need tea to do it, which I already gave up."

10. Valla

"They awaken in the same bed," said Mercy, "and their memories are momentarily confused."

"I work as a lab assistant for a scientist named Valla who is known for having very bad luck," said Hallamore. "My boss doesn't mind if I drop things or measure the wrong amounts because, he says, he's interested to see what effect my incompetence will have on the outcome of the experiment.

"We are performing an operation 'to see if talk can start from sex' (or is it sex from talk). He begins by drawing a dollar sign on his hand. . . .

"I prepare the coffee, I set up the day's experiment, I fill the rats's bottles with water, I grade the homework, I chew Valla's food for him—it hurts my mouth—I eat the soft food he chews for me, I wash the sheets that my other biology teacher will sleep in. . . .

"When Valla hanged himself, I 'translated' him. . . .

"I knew that Valla couldn't survive in a rat's body. But I thought that rats were due for a comeback because they had gotten such a bad rap."

"I couldn't imagine what the ocean looked like," I said. "It must be kind of like a lake, I thought. The other places in the novels (England, the Ivory Coast, Brazil, Singapore, the Malay Archipelago) sounded very much the same to me . . . the same as Cloquet, I mean.

"We lived in a town called Cloquet that had two paper mills. My biology teacher worked at one of them. . . . The whole town smelled of sulfur. It was enough to make you gag sometimes. You couldn't eat, you didn't want to breathe; every breath was punishing. You went on a hike to escape it, you went swimming in the lake, but it was in the water and all over everything; you carried it with you."

11. Don Giovanni

"They awaken in the same bed," said Mercy, "and their memories are momentarily confused."

"Remember my first play?" I said. "A version of 'The Hound of the Baskervilles' for children; I was the hound."

"I remember," said Hallamore. "The newspaper said that you captured the 'naïve insouciance' of the hound."

"On his report card, the biology teacher complained of his incessant baying," said Mercy. "But already he had seduced everyone with his hound costume, its glossy coat and soft paws."

"My failings as an actor," I said. "Forgetting my lines, missing my cue, entering on the wrong side of the stage; or else speaking my line twice, forgetting individual words, or saying the right words with a strange intonation. Will I never make it through a performance without doing something wrong?"

"You were making three-hundred-and-fifty dollars a night at the Guthrie," said Hallamore. "Your only responsibility, it seemed, was to douse the candles at the end of the first act in 'Cyrano.' I believe you put yourself through college that way."

"In pantomime class," said Mercy, "Wendy Lehr made the following sarcastic remarks: 'Don't check your smile in the mirror, Don.' 'Pantomime is the SILENT art, Don.'"

"My failings as a comedian," I said. "Dropping the ball, dropping the flower, falling over the cliff, drowning in the pool."

"And you had written a play," said Hallamore, "in which one of the characters said something like: 'You are either insane or crazy, or perhaps a combination of the two!'"

"He was interested in a photograph of Bain Boehlke," said Mercy. "The one that showed him cradling a duck in his arms."

"You were bored by any script that you knew by heart," said Hallamore, "and because you were also a gifted writer, you would write new dialogue for yourself. Often the lines you invented were a kind of commentary on the lines they replaced in the original script. For instance, in a production of 'State Fair,' by Rodgers and

Hammerstein, you altered the line 'sitting in the kitchen, talking to women,' to 'I can no longer pronounce the word "women" naturally.'"

"Some of the theatrical pieces in which I performed," I said. "'He Who Gets Slapped,' 'Bus Stop,' 'Woyzeck,' 'She Stoops to Conquer,' 'The Invitation,' 'Getting Out of Bed without Using the Stomach Muscles.'"

"In another play," said Mercy, "they were going to shoot him out of a cannon."

"You were writing a play called 'The Invitation,'" said Hallamore, "and you used a stage direction that went: 'Their sigh brings them to the ground.'"

"Phil Eaton showed me a comic strip ('Blondie') in which his name appeared," I said.

"I remember," said Hallamore, "when you were trying to decide between the lines 'Gee?' and 'Huh' to end our production of 'Peter Pan.'"

"The curtain wouldn't go up," said Mercy, "so I went onto the catwalks and made the repairs with a ballpoint pen as my only tool."

"I remember a line spoken by the countess in 'Lulu,'" I said. "'I'll find my own way out.'"

"I remember the lighting technician told you you had no sense of timing," said Hallamore.

"What makes you think you are Don Giovanni," said Mercy, "delight and terror of ladies and husbands, enemy to all and father to none?"

12. The reproducibility of an emotion

"They awaken in the same bed," said Mercy, "and their memories are momentarily confused."

"Do you remember your dream?" I said. "You were bouncing a soccer ball off your knee. 'Hello there,' I waved to you, a wave that was almost obscene, which you misinterpreted (you thought I wanted to play too!); you passed the ball to me, and I more or less tripped over it, chased after it, couldn't control it, until you came to the rescue."

"You offered me a cigarette," said Hallamore, "which, to my surprise, I accepted. 'I've never done this before,' I said as you lit it for me, 'although I've been around cigarettes all my life!'"

"I don't feel refreshed," I said. "Is my name Hallamore? What a disturbing idea."

"No, I'm Hallamore, you're Willy," said Hallamore. "You're the fussy one, remember?"

"I'm willing to entertain the idea that my name is Hallamore," I said. "But how will we be able to tell which one of us is talking?"

"Wait," said Hallamore. "I'm hungry—"

"So maybe you're the one who's talking?" I said. "And I'm the one who wants to talk?"

"Food will solve this problem," said Hallamore. "What's the last thing you remember eating before going to bed?"

"I remember it as a kind of bread," I said, "a sweet bread made with a very thin, soft dough, some kind of paste between the layers of dough, a walnut paste. It made my mouth feel funny when I bit into it—like paper—and it gave me a little pain at the seam under my tongue."

"I remember it as a spiced meat called 'porketta,'" said Hallamore, "made, I suppose, with pork, which they used to put on sandwiches when I was a kid. My biology teacher ate them sometimes, and was always sick afterwards."

"How long does it take for a mind, severed from consciousness, to find its worry?" said Mercy. "Not very long, surely. You awaken, emerge from your bed, and it's as though your worries are laid out like a freshly pressed suit for you to wear. Or perhaps they are packed in a suitcase, placed helpfully at the foot of the bed so that you'll be able to put on the same worries in another city."

"Maybe the contents of this suitcase will tell us something about our past," I said.

"I don't see how it can help, since we don't know which one of us it belongs to," said Hallamore. "I think we are much more likely to learn something from the contents of our stomachs."

"There's nothing in here but pants and shirts," I said. "And here is a photograph of the young man in his shirt. He looks like you, Hallamore."

"You're wearing my shirt," said Hallamore.

"We have the same shirt!" I said. "So we might as well talk at the same time?"

"Someone has switched the laces on these shoes," said Hallamore. "But I shouldn't have been sleeping with my shoes in the bed anyway."

"Or does your mind continue to worry even in the absence of an object?" said Mercy. "Aren't you always worried, looking for some material for your worry to consume—or, actually, to worry?"

"My mind without worry would be untethered," said Leah Gelpe. "And it would worry: 'What,' it would say, 'is the source of my worry?'"

"Even the unconscious mind will find its worry," said Mercy. "You awaken in your dream and the bed has become your enemy: it tries to shake you out onto the floor, collapses on you, picks itself up, folds itself double, and collapses again, trying to crush you with its weight."

"Or, in your dream," said Leah Gelpe, "you awaken on your back. Voices. Laughter. You put out your hand, and somewhere behind you it discovers a semihard dick. You open your eyes. Two boys are kneeling by your head; one of them is spitting up milk."

"Or you awaken," said Mercy, "out of your dream, and on the wall next to your head there's an area of stress: the paint cracks, bubbles, flakes, discolors. This is the place where your unconscious

I liked to run and leap, so they put me on the playing field.

mind was projecting its worry during its vacation from reality."

"My vacation? It was Chekhov," said Hallamore. "Bad Chekhov. An untenanted reality."

"Reality includes 'vacation,'" I said. "Thank you, reality, for including me. Thank you for sending me on tour."

"The bus ride was compulsory," said Hallamore. "The vacation was too."

"The bus ride was the highlight of my vacation," I said. "Thank you, Minneapolis, lacustrine city . . . "

"I exclude you (Willy) from my reality," said Hallamore. "A vacation from you. I had set aside an amount of money for this purpose: so that it could be enjoyed without letting you know about it. So that I wouldn't have to make a dent in the money that you knew I was carrying in our suitcase. Nonetheless there was a dent, which I could not account for. It appeared at just that moment, as I stepped down from the bus with a lie in my mouth, and in precisely the amount that I had set aside and secretly spent—as though the lie had cost an amount of money, as though the lie had cost exactly the amount I had failed to mention."

"If you unzip this compartment, you won't be able to take it back," I said. "If you open the letters in this compartment, you won't be able to put the envelopes back together so that they look unopened."

"We're not supposed to have these letters," said Hallamore. "I don't think we should read them."

"If we read these letters, we won't be able to forget them," I said. "If we take them out of their compartment, they won't fit back in."

"If we put these letters into a novel, then they could be duplicated," said Hallamore. "If we reproduced the novel, then we could share it."

"If you and I can share the same thing, then it doesn't exist," I said. "It's a novel that can't be reproduced."

"If you can have it and I can have it too," said Hallamore, "then it doesn't exist. It's an illusion. A newspaper that can't be understood."

"If we could put this feeling into a novel, then we might be able to reproduce it," I said.

"If this feeling could be put in a novel," said Hallamore, "you wouldn't be able to get it out again. What you wanted was the feeling, not the novel."

"The effect can't be reproduced," I said. "The idea can't be communicated. The experiment can be repeated but the result can't be recorded."

"Our story is too depressing to be told," said Hallamore. "If you can understand me, then I must be telling a lie."

"If this thing can be conveyed, then it doesn't exist," I said. "If you can understand me, then I'm hiding something. If it could be reproduced, that would make it less interesting."

"You and I know too much about one another," said Hallamore. "Too much for there to be any possibility of a conversation."

"You and I both depend on the other person in a conversation to perform a crucial action to keep the conversation going," I said. "So we can't talk to each other."

"Let's put all your things in a grapefruit box," said Mercy, "in order to forget them. So that they won't make you anxious. So that you won't have to worry about them anymore. So that you won't ever find them BY ACCIDENT."

"Programs," said Hallamore. "I saved them. I saved the old programs in a grapefruit box. Until they weren't there anymore. Until they disintegrated. Turned to ash."

"A prize essay on James J. Hill," said Mercy, "turned to ash. An award from the newspaper: turned to ash. A Jerome Fellowship, a McKnight Fellowship: lost, turned to ash."

"The spirit doesn't even know you," I said. "The spirit dies before it knows."

"The spirit wants to award money," said Hallamore, "to Renee Gladman."

13. The lost umbrella

"Describe your umbrella," said Leah Gelpe. "The lost article goes to the one who can describe it best, as though you could make an umbrella appear just by talking about it."

"I open my umbrella very carefully," said Mercy, "releasing the catch, peeling back the armature piece by piece, section by section, gently molesting the stem until everything locks into place and covers me. My umbrella is long, with red stripes; when I hold it up, I can't see anything above my waist but red stripes. When it's closed, I can swing it back and forth, making a path for myself wherever I go, sometimes taking flowers off their stems, sometimes impaling dead leaves and bits of trash on the spike at the end. When I close it up, splinters from the handle, which is bamboo, sometimes get under my fingernails; I can still feel them for days afterwards. And sometimes, when I return home, I have felt that the effort required to close my umbrella would be too much for me, so I leave it open.

"I found it one morning in my apartment. Hallamore was sleeping on the sofa (charming picture), and I didn't want to disturb him—'But,' I thought, 'I'll just take something of his so he'll know, when he gets up, that I saw him resting there.' At that moment the umbrella presented itself to my hands: it was sticking out of the cushions, and my brother's hand rested lightly on the handle. 'Ho-ho,' I chuckled, 'this would go well with my jacket,' and cheerfully appropriated it. 'But it's a woman's umbrella, so it can't belong to him anyway. Someone else must have left it,' and I brought it to work with me. 'Look what I have,' I told Leah Gelpe. 'That's disgusting,' she said, flipping out, 'you can't come to work dressed like that,' and after that I hid it in my apartment and never took it out again, until one day it wasn't there anymore, and I've always assumed that the person it belonged to in the first place must have come by to reclaim it."

"I found my umbrella in Mercy's apartment," I said, "behind the sofa. 'Oh, this is the most comfortable sofa in Minneapolis!' I said, just so that there would be something to say, and I leaned back a little farther to show that I had been completely seduced by the sensuous pleasure imparted to my shoulders by the cushions. 'But I must get out of here!' I said, but it seemed to me that I could not leave yet because no one had heard me. 'It's hard to leave because your sofa is so comfortable!' I had let my arm, at about this time, dangle over the arm of the sofa—overdoing it because I sensed that no one was paying attention. That was when the umbrella fell into my hand. I didn't realize at first that it was an umbrella because the stem not only collapsed but fitted together at the ends into a hoop; in its nylon pouch, it looked more like a hat. 'But who wears a hat?' I said to no one in particular, and carried it home under my arm.

"I lost my umbrella in the street on a rainy day when I ran into Hallamore; he had no umbrella and was completely drenched. 'Isn't that my umbrella you have there? I've been looking for it for ages.' 'No, no,' I started to say, 'this isn't yours,' but he had already taken it out of my hand and thanked me. Soon he was progressing up the street with his peculiar mechanical gait, swinging his legs far out ahead of him; he had left the umbrella open but was not taking care, as far as I could see, to keep its dome over his head. I stood for a moment in the rain and watched him go."

"My umbrella is a perfect novel," said Hallamore, "because it gives everyone a chance to talk and because no one can read the entire thing; except that it has no title, my umbrella is a perfect novel. 'What will you live on?' say the gods and spirits to me. 'I will live and have power through bread.' 'Where will you live?' 'I will live in my sister's apartment on Colfax Avenue and sleep on her sofa at night and go out in the day. My umbrella stripes the day with disbelief, and I no longer need or want any other . . . umbrella. . . .'"

"It finally happened," said Mercy. "Hallamore was talking and talking, and he fell asleep."

"The winner!" said Leah Gelpe.

"I win!" said Hallamore. "What did I win?"

"A loaf of bread," said Mercy. "The breadwinner!"

"There must be some mistake!" said Hallamore. "I really don't deserve it!"

14. The easy winners

"This fine bread goes to you, Hallamore," said Leah Gelpe, "in recognition of your unerring instinct for choosing the wrong word. Through the years, even when you had to speak briefly, you have invariably managed to use a word that no one could make any sense of, and you always thought that you were terribly clever for thinking it up. Your shining example challenges the rest of us to express ourselves more obliquely, to use words that obscure rather than clarify our intentions—we who typically use a few words over and over. We don't even like them especially, but they are the only words we can remember."

"He's eating the bread from the wrong end," said Mercy. "And I want to correct his mistake, take the thing out of his hand, turn it around. But I also don't want to embarrass him further."

"Wonderful bread," said Hallamore. "Mercy, you must try some. It's real soft . . . and it's sweetened with nutritious molasses."

"No, thanks, I'm zoophagous," said Mercy.

"Won't you have some, Willy?" said Hallamore.

"Your desire to share the bread shows that it doesn't really belong to you," I said, "because if it were really your bread, how could you bear to see it divided?"

"You've been disqualified, Hallamore," said Leah Gelpe. "Your prize has been revoked."

"I've already eaten some of it," said Hallamore.

"So much the worse for you," said Leah Gelpe.

"Oh Hallamore," said Mercy, "I would rather have you at the height of your powers. I will never forget the day my biology teacher took me aside and said, 'Young lady, listen to me: No one will like you if you let them see that you like Hallamore. If you want to get anywhere on this little planet you will have to conceal your love for your brother like a deformed limb. In certain circles, it is impossible to pronounce the name Hallamore without eliciting roars of laughter. They call him soft-brained because he never fails to bring out as a last-ditch defense that precious softness of his, which he once brandished before the senate in an attempt to salvage his lost and ruined reputation, shouting over everyone's laughter: "Mr. President, I want softness, I want softness!"—as, shuffling our feet noisily, we filed out of the auditorium.'"

"As I followed the others out of the auditorium," I said, "I called over my shoulder, 'I will never abandon you, Hallamore!' I know he is somewhat ridiculous. He tends to make mistakes with the dictionary, especially with big words, and gets himself into tangles that he can never get out of. Listen to the way he says the word 'extraordinary' and you'll see what I mean. 'Ex-straw-dinary!' But how can I bring myself to abandon him? He saved me from the grim monodrama of the restaurant. Without Hallamore, you get monodrama. With Hallamore, you get method, and dialectic."

"That which is sweet should be avoided," said Mercy. "Hallamore is sweet, and I will not taste him; Hallamore, I will not consume you, and I will not tread on you with my sandals.

"Open to me, earth; I despise Hallamore and will not taste him; I have not gone infected into Minneapolis. I will not touch what you touch, twice-hated Hallamore; my body revolts against what Hallamore produces; my biology teacher slept all the way through Hallamore's production of *The Three Sisters*.

"Woe to Minneapolis! You pick over the bodies of the dead; you turn the color of your food. What you have eaten is Hallamore; you are the yolk and the shell of the same egg, and I will not be subdued by my enemies. What I double-detest, I will not taste; what I detest is Hallamore, and I will not taste him; what my biology teacher detests is Hallamore, and he will not enter into my body. I will not hold you in my mouth, break for you into a bowl, or flow for you into a basin. I will not go upside-down for you."

15. At the Sri Lanka Curry House

"You turn your slide projector off," said Mercy.

"When I see you," I said, "I turn off my slide projector. Everything I want to throw at you returns to me. All the materials I want to apply to you come unstuck. I throw down my tools. The light goes out."

"The image of yourself that you project," said Mercy, "to illuminate the world, devolves. It cancels itself out."

"I don't exist," I said, "I cancel myself out. Reduced to nothing, a sheet of paper, I tear myself into bits, I undo myself. When I see you, I want to remove every trace of myself from my surroundings. To make it impossible for anyone to follow me."

"You scan my face," said Mercy, "looking for something you can recognize, looking at it in a way that makes it burn."

"I have no idea what he sees," said Hallamore. "His vision is terrible, but he doesn't wear his glasses. That's why he mistakes you for someone else."

"How could I have mistaken you for Minneapolis?" I said. "I had noticed that one city seemed to hide another, that Minneapolis seemed to be somewhere behind every city, because it was the grid on which my mental picture of any city was drawn, so that my mind had a way of drawing on its knowledge of Minneapolis when I didn't know where I was. That's why the edges of everything seemed a little fuzzy, as though I was looking at a photograph of something that had shifted during a long exposure, and everything seemed a little to one side of where it should have been: because I was projecting one city onto another. That's why I saw your face as a map of Minneapolis: because that's the only image that's left when every light is dimmed."

"The reason why I mistook you for Minneapolis," said Mercy, "is that you had a tendency to disappear into the woodwork, like a city that blends into another, so that a person could never be sure, when talking to you, whether she was addressing you or a defect in her vision, a smudge on the lens of her glasses."

"Distances seem much greater in an unfamiliar city," I said. "And you seem far away from me."

"You always want to dissociate yourself from the environment," said Mercy. "You make it impossible for anyone to reconstruct your motives."

"When I see you, I always want to run away," I said. "And I want to remove all labels, thereby decommercializing the objects around me. To leave behind no item that can be identified as 'mine.'"

"You show up," said Mercy, "and I don't remember because it's been so long. Everything reminds me of something else."

"When I see you," I said, "I hate myself with my whole self. I want, when I see you, to eliminate every trace of my project. To be erased. Cancelled. Undone. Submerged. When I see you, I am completely wretched and want to be filtered until I come out clean. To leave nothing behind me. To emerge whole. To pass through."

"When I see you," said Mercy, "I want to live in well-designed 'surroundings' (ominous word)."

"Love is around you," I said. "A veil of emotions, your own and others's, surrounds you. Through a cloud of intricate designs, I want to enlighten you. To uncloud you. To dispel the fog. But other loves surround you."

"Together we make a whole person," said Mercy. "Our knowledge makes a complete history. The sum of our opinions is the truth."

"The entire history of our friendship is implicit in this moment," I said. "We can't go any further (at least, not in this direction). Nothing more can be made of this. Nothing you say can make this new."

"We are left," said Mercy, "with the reality of our project."

16. Next slide, please!

"I had heard stories about Mercy," I said. "That she was violent. That was what drew me to her. I saw her get into a fight once. What I disliked wasn't her aggression, it was her sentimentality. This wasn't immediately apparent; you had to spend some time with her, let her talk for a while, before something came out of her mouth that was really corny. Sentiment was the motive behind all her aggression; her violent acts were committed in this spirit."

"You always think you're the one who depends on the other," said Hallamore. "Then the opposite turns out to be true."

"It's hard to say who makes the decisions," I said. "You think you know, but it's not who you think. I thought I was the one who depended on her, but that turned out not to be true. I was making the decisions before I turned them over to her. I'm still making the decisions."

"I'm haunted by you," said Mercy.

"You can't be haunted by a living person," said Hallamore.

"You can't be haunted by a restaurant," I said.

"Well," said Hallamore, "you can be haunted by a meal that didn't, so to speak, agree with you."

"Can you be haunted by something you ate a long time ago," I said, "in your childhood?"

"Can you be haunted by a bakery?" said Mercy. "You can 'haunt' a restaurant, of course: you can order the same food every time until they anticipate you and tell you what you want before you get a chance to open your mouth—'The usual?'—and you feel slightly embarrassed because you realize you're in sort of a rut. You can 'frequent' a restaurant until it becomes an experience that can't be ruined by anticipation, until it becomes the only restaurant for you, until you find yourself standing in front of it when you hadn't even decided where you were going, until the manager says hello and your name when you come in and you say hello to the waiters and chefs when you see them on the street, because it's as though you work there too, until you start to think of them as kind

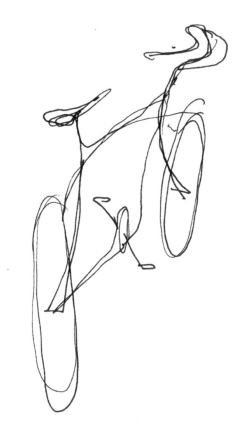

Something about a bicycle.

of like your family and one of them as your sister for example, until you start to dream about eating there (can you be haunted by a dream?), until the restaurant closes and you get no pleasure from your memories of it, and the dreams aren't very satisfying either because you never get to eat more than a few bites. I must have some more of that food!"

"We can't afford it," I said. "Besides, food doesn't taste good in an artificial environment. But it always looks so good in movies, books, and paintings."

"It always looks good," said Hallamore. "I like to think of you, Mercy, back in our old haunts of antique wonder and youthful excess. I remember you standing by the massive double door of the restaurant—the door of the Curry House, which is shaped like a mouth—with your hand on the doorknob, like two mouths. I imagine: and we are magically transported into the restaurant, as if in a dream. . . . Perhaps we will never eat that food again."

"But it is still here," I said. "The chairs are pulled up to the tables, the tables are set with silverware carefully wrapped in cloth napkins, the places are set with enormous plates, chunky glasses, menus—as though you might sit down and eat there. When you peer inside you can almost see yourself sitting at one of the tables, your former self, enjoying a meal."

"I knew immediately that Willy was in the restaurant," said Mercy, "because I found my own bicycle chained outside. He is probably the last person you should give your bicycle to, a danger to himself and to others, a walking mind-body problem. . . . Willy, that jacket does not fit you."

"Don't sit here," I said. "You're interrupting a private conversation between me and my biology teacher. This dinner is his way of asking me to visit him in Miami."

"I've never met your biology teacher," said Hallamore. "Is that his jacket?"

"He's in the men's room," I said. "You'd like him."

"I like him," said Mercy. "He gave me a ride once, only I couldn't find my way home from where he dropped me, so I got back in the car and went home with him. You say he's your teacher,

Willy, but he's not a bit like you."

"Yeah, well, I'm not certified to teach biology," I said.

"The funny thing," said Mercy, "was when I stopped by his house the next time I was in the neighborhood, only you were living there."

"Housesitting," I said.

"When the overpowering smell of spices fills the air, I'm positive that Natasha will regain consciousness," said Hallamore. "The smell of delicious food will bring her out of her trance. Should we order for her? What would she like, do you think?"

"What does one get here?" said Mercy. "Everything looks good."

"I always get the curry noodles," I said. "Hallamore always gets the lamb roti—but it's not their best dish."

"I have this absurd habit," said Hallamore, "of wrapping my napkin around my silverware in a complicated shape. Sometimes before I see what I've done, the knot is so tight that I can't get at the things inside. Oh Willy, I see I've done the same thing to your silverware as well."

17. A page left blank by intention

"As I sat down to write," I said, "a flea jumped on the paper. The flea was visible because the page was blank."

"A blank space is never the result of chance," said Hallamore. "As I was about to start eating, a flea jumped on the plate. The flea was visible because the plate was empty."

"A flea appeared at the center of the dinner table," I said. "It appeared to rise to the surface of the table from unseen depths; as it skipped along, it appeared to be carried from one place to another by little waves in the tablecloth. Most likely it had jumped from my arm, which I now removed from the edge of the table. The flea made no sound when it landed. Nor was it possible to determine precisely where on my body it had come from."

"I was sure that the flea had come from my body," said Mercy. "My body was covered with red marks in places where the flea had taken blood, especially on the legs. The flea always seemed to start at the ankles, working its way up from there. Every night it got a little farther up. Now it was up to my chest. There were some marks at shoulder-level."

"It did not feed on me," I said, "except at night, as far as I could tell. I could never find it on my body during the day."

"I had never seen a flea," said Mercy, "until one appeared on my plate. Suddenly I recognized it as the source of my displeasure and understood that it was not the only one; there were many more fleas than the one I saw; it represented others and belonged to a community just as I belonged to a household, a city, a nation. I knew that they were there because of the red marks that I saw on myself and believed that they had been introduced into the apartment through the agency of the dog, who, I knew, sometimes liked to unburden himself of the cares of his life by lounging on the bed in the middle of the day."

"I was so touched," said Hallamore, "by the wistful expression on his face at these times that I was unable to deny him this pleasure."

"I no longer took any pleasure in sleep," I said, "because it had to take place in bed, and I tended to put it off for hours into the night, pacing around the room and fingering the marks that the flea had left, until I absolutely could not stay awake any longer and I could almost hear my feet saying 'to bed' as I walked on them. When, with great misgivings, I had finally deposited myself in the bed, I still could not sleep although I needed it badly, kept lurching out of bed, feeling a little pain, wanting a light to see it by."

"At first," said Mercy, "the marks were hardly visible against the skin because they were almost the same color. The marks were bumps that lifted out of the skin and sometimes itched like hell; at other times they hardly itched at all. There seemed to be a rule that at any time no more than two of the places where the flea had taken blood could really itch. One of them would itch like hell, another would itch just a bit, and the rest would not itch at all unless you applied something to them, such as a hot washcloth, which afforded some relief by concentrating the itch to an unbearable degree."

"When they itched," said Hallamore, "you thought that the flea was biting you again, and you pulled your sock down to see if the flea was there, but it had bitten you hours ago, although it hadn't bitten you in the way that you might take a bite out of some small thing: It had made a wound and inserted itself in the wound."

"Then the marks turned red," I said. "It was not scratching them that made them red, because they seemed to do that whether you scratched or not. The marks had to change color several times before they could fade away."

"They had to pass through several shades of red," said Mercy, "until they turned purple. When they turned purple they flattened out and faded away. They gave the impression of being purple, but actually they were a network of irregular dark lines on a faint red ground. At this point they looked awful, worse than before, but they didn't itch."

"As I put my naked hand on the table, three fleas are seen to appear on it," said Hallamore. "Shocked, I withdraw my hand."

"A slight pain, a whisper," I said, "something in the area of the navel, not on the navel, but on the rim of it. Almost on the surface, and it can mean only one thing: A flea is crawling over your belly."

"Suddenly you realize that you have been bitten by a flea," said Hallamore. "Hard to say when it happened."

"Unable to excuse myself from the delightful conversation at the dinner table," said Mercy. "That unmistakable feeling again. A hand slipped discreetly under my jacket. Giving the front of my shirt a thoughtful rub. Flapping one hand against my stomach in a way that might dislodge the flea but surely would not injure it. Excuse me."

"Alone in the bright bathroom," I said. "Before the mirror. Passing a hand thoughtfully over my chest. Opening the shirt from the top. Putting myself in the light."

"Finished," said Mercy. "The check is brought; I place my card on it; the check is removed; and returns, in an altered form. As I start to write my name, a flea appears on the paper. It must have jumped from my writing arm onto this small square of paper on which I was about to write."

"It crawls from one end of the paper to the other," said Hallamore. "It appears to be carried over the paper by currents in the air, like a flake of ash. It almost seems to be glowing."

This page intentionally left blank.

18. A better novel compared with a more beautiful one

"Poor Natasha!" said Mercy. "And she's so talented. . . . I could get her a job at my work—whipping meringues, for instance. . . ."

"You're still working at Gelpe's?" I said. "I went there yesterday and was sure it would no longer exist. But it was open. Today I returned assuming that it would still be open. But it no longer existed."

"I had the same problem with your sister," said Mercy. "One time I was in the neighborhood I dropped by her place and found you there. Another time I was waiting for you outside your house, and she came out instead."

"We traded houses," I said.

"Natasha is so interesting," said Mercy. "Is she named for the character in the Anthony Powell novel?"

"What is she made of?" said Hallamore. "Some special material . . ."

"Something that doesn't scuff," I said. "When you rub it, it starts to glow all over, not just in the place where you're rubbing."

"What is Natasha's dream?" said Hallamore. "What does it consist of? The dream of a perfect society?"

"No dream could make you wait this long for a meal," said Mercy.

"No dream could invent such a complicated menu," I said.

"No dream," said Hallamore, "could bring all my favorite people together like this."

"In a dream," I said, "my foot would not be asleep, or I would not realize that it was."

"Willy," said Mercy, "do you realize that the women in your novels are always being raped?"

"Willy doesn't see that as a problem," said Hallamore, "because there are no women in his novels."

"Do you mean because the characters are all men?" said Mercy. "Or because fictional characters have no sex?"

"I'm not sure that there are characters in his novels," said

Hallamore.

"Rape is a problem in the novel," I said, "as it is in Minneapolis (but not a social problem)."

"But, I mean," said Hallamore, "if crime is on the rise in the novel and not in Minneapolis . . ."

"Doesn't Minneapolis include the novel?" said Mercy. "Have you ever read a novel? How do you know that what you're writing is novels?"

"What do you want when you want to write a novel?" said Hallamore. "Is it a desire to create poetry? A feeling that uses language?"

"What is it you want when you want a pastry?" I said. "Is it the pastry you want or the feeling of eating it? Or is it the feeling of having eaten and being wonderfully full? Or is wanting a pastry not directed at any object? Only a feeling that uses sugar to fulfill itself?"

"What do I want when I see you?" said Mercy. "Do I want to throw myself at you, give you a playful shove, or even tackle you? Is this desire focused on a discrete part or accessory of or to you, such as the back of your neck or the collar of your shirt? As though it would be enough just to put my hand there? Is it possible that my intentions can be discerned in my face, in what I do with my hands, in something I've said? Because you're giving me a look that says, unmistakably: 'Do not molest me.'"

"If you were a fictional character," I said, "you wouldn't be realistic."

"If you were a fictional character," said Mercy, "you would be the heroine of a nineteenth-century novel."

"If you were a fictional character," I said, "you would be independently wealthy."

"If you were a fictional character," said Mercy, "you wouldn't have to worry about money."

"All your sentences," I said, "are made of two pieces of wood connected by a hinge."

"Your sentences have the shape of an umbrella," said Hallamore.

"Your sentences are completely unlike one another," said Mercy. "She turned the tape over and played it again. She reversed the tape and played it again. This is something we can all relate to."

"No novel could capture the beauty of my sister," said Hallamore, "as she eats an apple. Is her beauty enhanced by what she is eating?"

"A delicate beauty," I said, "because everything else about her is indelicate and threatens to destroy her beauty."

"What does the apple add to the delicate quality of her beauty?" said Hallamore. "Does it reassert what she is saying in apple-language? Does its shape or color correspond to what she is wearing? No one would think her beautiful, or even pretty, if she had no apple or if she had eaten the flesh of the apple and was left with the core to dispose of. Who would think her pretty if I were to take her apple away?"

"No novel could depict Hallamore's extraordinary pettiness," I said, "in taking that apple away from his own sister."

"Your sister is practically in a vegetative state because your novels are so boring," said Hallamore. "How do you know she isn't already dead? And what have you done to your biology teacher that prevents him from completing a bowel movement?"

"My theory is that Willy doesn't know the first thing about writing a novel," said Mercy. "He pretends that he is a writer or that he has written something, but obviously he isn't writing novels, he's producing a more potent sleep-inducing object. He's probably the most distinguished producer of sleeping aids in this country, only he doesn't know it! Do you ever hear him talking about novels except for the ones he's, for lack of a better word, writing? Have you ever actually seen him reading a book? Does he even know how to read? Try it, test him—Willy, tell me, what's your favorite novel? (He picks up his fork and directs it toward his mouth, then stops and stares, apparently dismayed to observe that there is nothing attached to it.) Name a novel you've read in, say, the last five years. (He looks down at his plate, which is empty, not a crumb on it; carefully, with an appearance of great effort—'Please, do not disturb me, this is hardly the time'—he draws his finger across it to pick up a trace of an imaginary sauce.) Define 'novel.' (His mouth churns feebly, as though he is chewing something, and he tries to meet my gaze, tries to give me a look—'Please, I'm chewing, can't this wait?'—and he can't manage it; finally he has to swallow, then he glances anxiously at my plate, at Hallamore's, at Natasha's, and they're empty; almost in a frenzy, he looks all around the room, at the other tables, as though he might find something edible on one of them, and they are bare and unused, no one is sitting around them; he tries to get the waiter's attention, to ask for something that he'll think of when the waiter answers his call, but there is no waiter; out the window, across the street, at the Y, there is nothing to merit his attention, only some confused-looking people exercising in the window, and they seem to be staring back at him thoughtfully, as though they might start shouting out questions about how he conceptualizes the novel's form and function.) No, really, why don't you tell me what a novel is? . . . Come on, tell me, because I'd really like to know! (With a worried look applied to his face, he grasps the base of his water glass, but there is nothing in it; the water pitcher is also empty.) I'm dying to know: What do you think a novel is? How can you tell that something is a novel and another thing is not? What unique qualities would the novel-thing have? (He is really starting to panic! With nothing on the table to distract him, how will he be able to avoid answering my question? How did this conversation start, anyway? He tries to recall: How did he get himself into this? Because he definitely never wants it to happen again.) So: 'novel,' textbook definition. I'm waiting . . . (He gives you a marvelous opportunity to examine him when he looks away. You get to watch the answer appear in his head and watch him move away from it.) What novel do you most admire? (He shifts to wipe his nose, sniffs, the chair groans, and each of these actions seems to express an indefinable sadness, but none of them is intended to.) Go on, tell me the plot of one novel."

". . . plot?" I said.

"You're not familiar with the term?" said Mercy. "Why don't you just admit it: The dogs on the street don't think you're worth barking at because you can't read!"

"A novel," I said. "It is a thing . . . made of words. . . ."

"I have been trying to discover what his conception of the novel is," said Mercy. "With no success! He wasn't able to describe the plot of a single novel. He couldn't even name one."

19. Novelization

"Novel," said Hallamore. "An object of pleasure."

"Novelism," said Mercy. "A discredited ideology."

"Novelist," said Hallamore. "One who subscribes to it."

"Novelization," I said. "Becoming a novel."

"Take this menu," said Mercy. "Turn it into a novel."

"For that I need a pencil," I said.

"Use whatever you normally use," said Mercy. "Whatever you normally do, do. Show us how happy it makes you."

"But I don't write novels in order to obtain happiness," I said.

"What are you going to put in your novel?" said Hallamore. "Try to put everything you know about candy bar machines in it. You could write it with a candy bar . . . and the words might come out coated in chocolate."

"There are lots of things you could put in it," said Mercy. "There are trees. There are people. The chalk is white. The sun is shining. None of these things is true."

"The big boy," said Hallamore. "The dark boy. The boy with the hat. A cut lip. Funny. Huh. Kind of a funny boy. Very dark. A little dark. Not a very nice boy. Talk this way all the time, and you won't have problems."

"The sentences were better when they were fragments," said Mercy. "Now they are full of holes where the fragments used to be."

"The sentences were better when there were two of them," said Hallamore.

"There's no hope," said Mercy, "for this sentence. There's no hope."

"He wrote five sentences," said Hallamore, "with one word. At the end of the day he still had not eaten."

"I started to write before I knew what it was going to be," I said. "Now I regard it with an expression of horror."

"Night became morning before he wrote another one,"

said Mercy. "The face of the page underwent a terrible change from morning to night, then no change at all between night and morning."

"How do you measure the distance between the two," said Hallamore, "when distance is measured in months, seasons, and generations? Was it the same as the distance between himself and the menu? The distance between his pencil and the menu? The distance from one end of the pencil to the other? The length of one of the creases in the menu?"

"I write a lot of sentences that don't lead to others," I said. "I know that I haven't always improved as I've gotten older."

"His hand cast a shadow over what he wrote," said Hallamore. "In the shadow the word 'perhaps' could be discerned."

"In trying to smooth the menu, he tore it in half," said Mercy. "He put the pencil in his mouth and the pencil dissolved."

"Again I follow the flea across the paper," I said. "The sentences got longer and I kept writing 'I' as though it were the only word."

"He wrote five novels," said Hallamore, "with one wolf. But the wolf was illegible, always came out looking like another wolf, never like itself."

"A page filled with wolves doesn't make a novel," said Mercy. "What good is a novel if it doesn't have characters?"

"A novel is just wolves on a page," I said, "and blanks between one wolf and another; the spaces between them can also be counted. It takes more than a nitwit to draw a blank."

"I love it," said Hallamore. "It's totally right-brain."

"What makes you think his brain had anything to do with it?" said Mercy. "It takes more than a lone wolf to make a novel. If there are no persons left, what's in it for you?"

"A lot of the wolves in a novel don't count," said Hallamore. "When you count them up, you find there was only one."

"So many novels, and hardly a wolf in them," said Mercy. "The question becomes, when do you add a second wolf? The question becomes, can the page be saved?"

"It takes a lot of wolves to make a novel fail," I said. "The novel gets lost in a cloud of wolves."

"When wolves fail, the page can only follow," said Hallamore. "Your novel becomes a crust of itself."

"It's ten o'clock," said Mercy. "Do you know where your wolves are?"

"Well, gee, they told me they were going to the library," I said.

"It's ten o'clock, and they're kicking you out of the restaurant," said Mercy. "They're turning out the lights."

"The library is closing," said Hallamore. "In fifteen minutes the circulation desk will be closed."

"The Curry House has no library!" said Mercy.

"Circulation desk is already closed," said Hallamore.

"The lie-bury, because that's where the lies are buried," I said. "The lie-berry, because that's where the lies bear all their fruits."

"On the street outside the Curry House, you're struck down by an invisible car," said Hallamore. "You don't realize it and continue walking."

"We buried him in the parking lot," said Mercy, "behind the restaurant."

"And published a volume of poems in his honor," said Hallamore.

20. Butter-side down

"He rose from the dead and invoked an unseen power," said Hallamore. "At the end of the day he still had not eaten. He said a spirit commands us—"

"He wouldn't shut up about the unseen power he represented," said Mercy. "He couldn't stop himself from talking about what he was thinking about."

"I'm calling to see if you're still interested in using the title *Fed-Exing the Bread?*" I said. "The title was changed for publication in a magazine and disseminated in an altered form, so am I to understand that you officially withdraw your interest in the title *Fed-Exing the Bread* as the title for a novel? And do I have your permission to claim it for myself for the purposes of ownership, reproduction, and other uses?"

"He rose from the dead and drank a gallon of coffee," said Hallamore, "without speaking, stepped out of his grave—and gave the novel a title."

"Isn't it true," said Mercy, "that he wanted to be given a title himself? To have a title bestowed on him?"

"He had composed more than fifty titles for the novel but could not tell which one described it best," said Hallamore. "Everyone called him something else because they did not know his title. They did not know how many titles he had."

"And you had only one idea," said Mercy. "You could hear the words as they were starting to appear. They were forming on the sidewalk and you could almost hear them. A novel forming on the sidewalk outside the restaurant."

"It sounded like the ice cover breaking up on a lake," said Hallamore. "The sound of the words taking form was like the sound that ice makes during a thaw when it breaks apart."

"We seem to see ourselves walking in the cold air," I said. "What vision has sprung up before us? The novel is calling to you across the ice. How will it make itself known to you?"

"She read it over and told him it was no good," said Mercy.

"She has dedicated her life to every kind of pleasure, likes to watch movies late at night, until the morning paper arrives, then she sleeps in the uneven light of the T.V., and wakes up with the newspaper in her lap."

"She hardly wears anything now," said Hallamore, "except for her bathrobe, which she never washes, and the tattered boxer shorts that she lifted from the 'discarded' pile at the laundry. Once in a while she goes out to deposit the royalty checks that she receives for the novel. He still has not found a suitable title for it."

"They surround themselves with objects of pleasure," I said. "Instruments that can be used to attain it (is television an instrument of feeling?), things that are pleasant to listen to, objects that are a pleasure simply to have in one's possession."

"I took the novel out of his hands," said Mercy, "before he could give it another title. I place before me objects of every kind of pleasure. I place before me *The Fatal Glass of Beer*, an old movie that I've seen many times."

"The movie is shown," said Hallamore. "It is not luminous."

"Natasha retrieved the novel from the 'discarded' pile," I said. "And filled it with things that she loved: pastries, cigarettes, conversations, the T.V., the newspaper, the telephone, various other novels. . . . Then she left out the telephone because it rarely gives pleasure."

"For obvious reasons," said Hallamore, "she left out things like the telephone. Her reasons for including cigarettes are less obvious because she does not smoke them and never intended to. Why does she care about them? How do they work in her mind?"

"She said goodbye to the pleasures of life when she put them in the novel," said Mercy. "Farewell, dream that suggests pastry; so long, reality-focusing conversation; goodbye, telephone that rings with painful accuracy. Because a novel is a repository of life's pleasures and can't actually give pleasure."

"As a novelist," said Hallamore, "you are expected to know the difference."

21. Weird scene

"Now we're on the subway," said Hallamore, "pretending not to see one another."

"This tunnel is too narrow," I said. "There's not enough room for truth."

"False!" said Mercy. "There's no subway in Minneapolis!"

"Yes, that's true," said Hallamore. "There's no truth in Minneapolis."

"There's not enough room for truth in the novel!" I said.

"Spoken falsely," said Mercy, "like a true novelist."

"There are deeper truths," said Hallamore, "that pass between cities in contraptions like the subway. This is a submerged truth."

"What is this truth submerged in?" I said. "Is it submerged in honey? Water? Molasses? Is it submerged in a jelly?"

"I am not afraid of this truth," said Mercy, "because it will never rise. It will not surface."

"This truth is submerged in a mild sauce," said Hallamore. "But it is a bitter truth."

"This truth doesn't scare me," said Mercy. "You cannot frighten me with this truth."

"If we are already submerged in the truth," said Hallamore, "we have no reason to fear."

"Minneapolis engulfs and separates us," I said. "Now we are truly submerged!"

22. Crossing the John Ashbery Bridge

"Three women are falling against one another," I said. "One of them stamps her foot and hugs herself to show how funny it is. I was the one who made them laugh. I said: 'I should charge you.'"

"But you said it in front of you and not behind you where we were laughing at you," said Mercy. "You kept pushing through the subway car, shoving your box in everyone's face: 'Five dollars, five dollars, five dollars . . .'"

"Cap of my pen disappears in the armpit of a man passing by," said Hallamore. "Something in the box he was swinging electrified the hair on my arms, and I looked up as he and his box sailed by. What did I see? My impression is that he was offering a set of architect's tools, mainly pencils, all different sizes. Or was it a collection of glass eyeballs? A bowl of porridge cushioned in velvet? Or ball bearings? The unresolved memory of what was in the box interposes itself between me and the page of the book where I have just read and underlined 'that we are in the middle of something immense, but at each moment we see only what is in front of us.' Alas! I can't see what's in front of me. I'm in the middle of an immense book but can't find my place in the book; can't recall what was in that chipboard box although I know that outside the box is this train; can't tell where the train is although I know it's somewhere under the city, in a hole whose contours I am unaware of."

"We're on the elevated train crossing the J.A. Bridge," said Mercy. "I'm in the middle of *Jane Eyre* but I understand that you are on the wrong train and have gone much further uptown than you intended."

"The Express, in which passengers stand together even more closely, is on the next track," I said. "What are they trying to express? They hold newspapers to their faces to show that they are in the middle of a newspaper rather than a crowded train."

"It sometimes happens," said Hallamore. "You get a closer look at another person than you would like in these situations.

Suddenly you find yourself staring into somebody's skull. But it's impossible to tell what a person reading a newspaper is thinking. On the Express you would have to stand right next to another person so that you were actually touching in several places, but you still wouldn't know what she was thinking."

"I take my brother's wallet and keys, and he doesn't notice until later," said Mercy. "It looks like I'm staring him in the face without really looking, but I see him all right; my attention is focused entirely on him as my hand, covered by *Jane Eyre*, searches in his pocket. It looks like I'm unaware of how close we are, that our faces are almost touching. The novel conceals this information: my hand, my proximity to another, my intense concentration."

"There's a tenderness to this scene," said Hallamore, "that can't be expressed in words."

"I put everything in my mouth," I said. "I mean, my novel."

You forget the unseen power that watches over the morning newspaper!

23. What is a newspaper?

"The newspaper," said Mercy, "is a device for concealing information. We look to the newspaper for information that we briefly hold onto, cherish, and let go: information that is hidden in the newspaper just as our faces and hands are hidden in it."

"What is usually concealed behind the newspaper is a face," said Hallamore. "But the newspaper actually gives you two faces: one of them is the newspaper itself, which is a mask; the other is your face regarding the newspaper, which is also a mask. The newspaper envelops you with a serenity that can't be challenged. When you hold a newspaper to your face you are practically not there, you are a piece of furniture . . . and the mask falls away only when you look up."

"I'm reading the newspaper so I don't have to talk to you," said Mercy, "holding it close to my face so I don't have to look at you, and I don't want to wonder about the nonsense they are printing in your newspaper either. When I gaze on my newspaper I'm lost to the world; I hold it over my head so that I can see only the newspaper."

"Even if you should happen to look up you would only see another newspaper," said Hallamore, "maybe not the same one, or not the same page, as the one you hold in your hands and wear as a mask."

"Maybe if we understood each other," I said, "we would sit together on the same bench and read the same newspaper. . . . No, when we really understood each other, there were no newspapers to hide behind."

"You're not hiding anything," said Mercy. "I know what you're looking at. You're easy to spot because you never change your newspaper; you've been using the same one for as long as I've known you. And you hold it upside-down. You probably wouldn't be able to read it anyway, though, because the pages are so brittle, yellowed, thin, and smudged that everything on them must be just obliterated. But the fact that you're holding it like that, so it's unreadable, shows you haven't really separated yourself from me and immersed yourself in it; you're only pretending to separate yourself so that you can monitor me closely."

"I'm looking for authentic culture," I said, "but can't find it in the newspaper."

"Here, try this newspaper," said Mercy.

"I feel dirty," I said. "No, I am dirty! It gets all over my hands."

"Dear cookie, you're such a mess," said Mercy. "You're a piece of rotten fruit. There's a great big rotten spot on your hand that goes all the way up your arm . . . and your neck, and the side of your head, and your ear is getting blacker; you're rotten before you're ripe! It's rotting your brain through your ear!"

"My fingerprints are all over the newspaper," I said, "and newsprint is on my fingertips. Now your fingerprints are on me too, and you're picking up some of the ink as well."

"We say," said Mercy, "that this or that 'touches.' The newspaper touches you and it costs about seventy-five cents."

"The price is not a secret," said Hallamore. "It is printed on every copy. The price is displayed so that it is likely to be the first thing one sees when one picks it up."

"The newspaper will always find me," I said. "Wherever I go and hide, it finds me. I can't get away from it, no matter what I do."

"Where the sidewalk narrows, the newspaper arrests your gait," said Hallamore. "From its machine, where the sidewalk collides with itself and slopes toward the street, the newspaper beholds you. It fixes you with its magnetic gaze. And you will not be able to continue on your journey until you have purchased a copy to take with you."

"The newspaper roams the streets while the city sleeps," I said. "Folded in the serene envelope of sleep, the city dreams the newspaper."

24. A serene envelope

"She didn't know whether she was on her back, her front, or her side," said Mercy, "or in what direction she had turned her face. She had no idea that the sheets held her in an unusual position, so that the shape of her body under the sheets and blankets would have looked like a crease in one of the blankets, because it was not a shape that the human body ordinarily likes to assume. It would have been impossible to determine whether or not there was a person in the bed without pulling back the blankets and searching under them.

"Her brother had pulled back the blankets and was looking at her expectantly. When he saw that she was only waiting for him to leave so that she could go to sleep, he started to talk in confused sentences. His voice rose as the sentences got more confused. His sentences were filled with improbable accusations; he accused her, among other things, of hoarding the newspaper, and even insinuated that she was concealing the newspaper somewhere in the room or on her body. He must have realized that it was not likely that she had done any of the things he was accusing her of, but this knowledge only seemed to fuel his anger: How could she have done something so strange, so false, so improbable? . . . It was outrageous. He went into the closet and pulled all her clothes off the hangers and cast them on the floor, ripping some of them in the process and scattering buttons across the floor. He did this with an odd flourish, as though ridding himself of a terrible burden, and he repeated the flourish a few times, because it seemed to please him. She did nothing to stop him, nor did she try to save the buttons. Then he yanked the drawers out of the dresser and, with the same violent gestures, unfolded the clothes and added them to the pile. He seemed to think that he was searching for a newspaper, but he was actually covering the floor with her clothes. She had not realized that she had so many clothes. She had often thought that she didn't have very many, that she had only a few things and as a result had to use a lot of ingenuity in dressing herself so that she didn't look the same every day, while other men and women were continually replacing everything in their wardrobes. Certainly she had never thought that the articles of clothing she owned would cover the bedroom floor. Some of them she had not worn in a long time; they no longer represented the kind of thing she liked to be seen wearing, or she had never worn them in the first place. There were also a few things she had worn in her childhood and was still holding on to—too small, probably, to contain more than a piece of the newspaper. They didn't look bad spread out on the floor like that; there were more colors in them than she might have anticipated. There were some books mixed in with the clothes, because her brother had transferred the contents of her small bookshelf onto the floor along with everything else, except that he had taken the books in his arms and set them down in a more or less deliberate arrangement, as he had always been careful when it came to handling books. Now he was wallowing in the mass of garments, unfolding everything that was folded and turning out the pockets, saying more to himself than to her, 'What have you done? Where is the newspaper?' 'It's in the envelope,' she started to say. 'What does that mean?' he said. 'I don't see an envelope.' 'The serene envelope,' she said, not very helpfully."

"Ensconced," said Hallamore, "in its serene envelope *(dans son enveloppe sereine)* . . ."

"Sort of a transferred epithet," I said, "because it isn't the envelope that's serene, it's the newspaper."

"Serenely ensconced," said Hallamore, "in its envelope . . . ensconced in its envelope of serenity . . . "

"The newspaper is delivered to the house," said Mercy. "Transferred from the plant to the truck, from the truck to the door, from the door to the kitchen. Every day the same thing: It looks the same, and maybe it gets a little worse. How could you tell? There are superficial differences in the wording, sure, differences that you might be able to make out if you examine it closely . . . comparing yesterday's with today's . . . until you have read the entire thing and wasted another day with the newspaper, until the newspaper comes to bed with you for your siesta and you comfort yourself with the illusion that you have made something out of it, when all you have made is a bed."

"Creating illusions in a world of appearances," said Hallamore, "the newspaper appears to be static. The pages have a certain solidity to them. They're divided into 'columns.' The words fit together so perfectly that the only empty space is at the outermost margin. And it appears to be saying only one thing. It says the same thing every day, in every section, every page, every part of the city . . . maybe it gets a little worse on every page. On one hand, it is constant; on the other, it is constantly changing. Then it isn't constant in any sense!"

"Now the story of the newspaper can be told," said Mercy. "Can it be told in the newspaper? No, because it is destroying itself all the time. Even the paper on which it is printed is made with an acid that eats paper. The newspaper has to be wrapped in plastic like something perishable, as though it couldn't stand the air outside its own bubble, as though it could breathe only the air that it itself gives off. It has to be wrapped in plastic like a cheese, on account of its great delicacy. When submerged in water it turns into pulp; it turns into dust if exposed to light; and it will disintegrate over time despite all precautions. If, for example, it comes into contact with human flesh, it disintegrates. That's why it has to be divided into sections for safekeeping, folded together, rolled up, reined in by a rubber band, wrapped in a bag of transparent plastic (which is not exactly an envelope). In this sheath it can't be molested, and its shape, that of a small loaf of bread, makes it easy to carry: It can be tucked comfortably under the arm, and when tossed lightly it will go all the way to your front door. But the folding and binding and wrapping make it somewhat difficult to get at the newspaper. Stripping it of its shell, I start to wonder, what is being protected, no, what am I being protected from? Is the newspaper so delicate? Or is there, instead, something in it that wants to get out? And is this layer of plastic enough to protect me from it?"

"But you do not formulate these questions," said Hallamore, "when you read the newspaper. The reader is above all serene. In its medium the newspaper suspends you where you stand reading on the narrowing sidewalk. Envelope serene! Oh syntax inverted! Oh serene epithet! Oh translated newspaper *(journal traduit)*!"

25. Newspaper buried in snow

"The reappearance of the newspaper in the morning," I said. "Its almost uncanny reappearance. The fact that it is delivered every day would seem to indicate that someone is continuing to pay the subscription. . . . But who?"

"The newspaper is delivered to your house like the mail," said Hallamore. "Nothing can stop it. Nothing can be done to prevent it."

"The newspaper is delivered to your house like an engraved invitation," I said. "An invitation to what? For whom?"

"The newspaper asks to be let inside," said Hallamore. "It arrives in the dead of night, like an illicit lover tapping at the screen. It waits patiently for you to extend an invitation."

"Go away, lover," said Mercy. "I'll meet you some other time."

"Soon enough, you find yourself missing the newspaper," said Hallamore, "checking to see if it has arrived, unable to sleep, then sleeping fitfully, dreaming of its arrival, waking to hear it pounding on the front door—"

"I went downstairs," said Mercy, "to look for the newspaper. I wanted to take it up to my room so that I could enjoy it without any distractions. I was jealous of anyone who also subscribed to the newspaper. I kept thinking about the other people who had it and how they related to it, where they lived, what they looked like. I knew that I did not have to share it, I had my own and could do anything with it, and I was prepared to do anything to make it divulge its secret. I was determined to make something of the newspaper, possibly a hat."

"You wanted to replace one language with another," said Hallamore. "To replace the newspaper with a small book."

"I wanted to make love to the newspaper," said Mercy. "I waited for it all morning. I waited for it exactly as Olivia de Havilland waits for Montgomery Clift in *The Heiress*. Finally I had to telephone the newspaper. The newspaper assured me that a newspaper would come. I ended up buying a copy of the newspaper at Kenny's

Market. Because it was Sunday the newspaper was somewhat more expensive . . . a great deal more expensive, in fact."

"The newspaper returns love," I said.

"Even the newspaper makes mistakes," said Mercy.

26. Does the newspaper intend violence?

"I have been watching the newspaper," said Mercy. "I believe it moves from time to time. I think it's moving toward the door. Does it intend violence?"

"For a centipede," I said, "the newspaper is an instrument of violence. If you ask the ghost of the dead centipede what a newspaper is, it will tell you: a device for eliminating centipedes."

"Maybe the newspaper commits violent acts without intending to," said Mercy. "Maybe it loves the centipedes and can only express its love with a sickening thud. Maybe it only wants to give them some shade or fan them a little as they go wobbling down the walls."

"The newspaper would like to destroy all the walls," said Hallamore. "When it crashes against the side of the house, it's thinking about the hole it would like to make. When you hear it pounding on the door, it's trying to knock it over."

"What are you doing to my house?" said Mercy. "Are you raining down like a potent classical god onto my little house?"

"I am throwing a newspaper at it," said Hallamore. "I have a job throwing newspapers at houses."

"Do you mind if I close the shade?" said Mercy.

"You don't like being seen by the paperboy," I said.

"Yes, it bothers me," said Mercy. "I don't really know why."

"Some things only the paperboy knows about you," I said. "He knows what you do when you're all alone. And he doesn't even know who you are and what your name is."

"Oh, he knows my name," said Mercy. "That is a secret I share only with the paperboy."

"He's flinging armfuls of newspapers at the house," I said. "He's battering the door with them. Will no one let him in?"

"I have a message concerning your house (contained in this newspaper)!" said Hallamore.

"What did he say?" said Mercy. "Does he intend violence?"

"I can't understand him," I said. "That's why I call him the newspaper."

"Is the newspaper having a deleterious effect on the outer wall of my house?" said Mercy. "Did he order a pizza? Is he holding a reception in front of my house?"

"He did not order the food because he was hungry," I said. "He thought he would read the newspaper, so he needed a bite to eat. When it turns out he is not going to read the newspaper, he leaves the food untouched."

"Why are there so many newspapers piled up in front of my house?" said Mercy. "Does the house produce them?"

I was too exhausted to answer. I had been out all morning, following the delivery truck, gathering the newspapers off the doormats. I thought that I was doing what I had been doing all along, now on a larger scale.

27. What is a newspaper? (2)

I slept for so long that I started to dream about waking up, getting
out of bed, putting on clothes, eating breakfast. My dream invented
problems that I might have, as though the only purpose of the
dream had been to perpetuate itself. If, for example, someone
were already in the shower; if someone were sleeping or having
a conversation in the room where I would be getting dressed; if
someone had taken my clothes and was in the process of putting
them on, someone I did not know very well and in whose presence
certain protocols would have to be observed . . .

I found myself entering the bedroom, the very room in which
I was sleeping as I dreamed this tiresome series of dreams, and
my only desire was to get into bed, not so that I could go to sleep,
but so that I could at last wake up. Instead I had to apologize for
waking Natasha, who had apparently been sleeping in the bed in
which I was actually sleeping as I apologized to her. Her presence
led me to doubt my original purpose in entering the bedroom:
Was I there, as I had supposed, so that I could sleep there, or was it
so that I could sleep with her, and whose idea was it that we would
sleep together, hers or mine? Now she was wearing glasses, which
was unusual for her, or so it seemed to me . . . unusual, anyway,
for a person who is supposed to be asleep. She wanted me to do
something for her now that she was awake, and proceeded to
explain to me a problem she had been having with her tooth. I did
not follow what she was saying, exactly, but finally understood that
she wanted me to bring her a plastic cup out of the bathroom, and
I got the idea that a tooth of hers was in that cup. I went out and
returned almost immediately . . . it was not clear, even to me, where
I had gone . . . and returned with something, possibly the cup, that
seemed to satisfy her. I could see that she was falling asleep, and
there was obviously no room for me in the bed, which only got
smaller every time I thought about it, so I told her goodnight. In
general, she was very solicitous throughout our brief conversation
and seemed delighted to see me, considering that I had disturbed

her rest. I told myself, as I shut the door as quietly as possible, at least I know where I find her.

When I finally woke up, I didn't know whether I had been sleeping or not. It seemed to me that I had not slept at all. It was still quite early in the morning, not long after I had gone to bed. The kid who delivers the morning paper had just slammed the door of his truck; now he was passing from one house to another, hurling newspapers at each one as he passed by. As he turned to face me I stepped away from the window. . . . I could not determine from the impression in the mattress whether I had slept or not. It appeared that I had fallen out of bed, only I didn't remember getting up from the floor . . . the sheets and blankets were in a tangle there . . . I suppose I could have kicked them off.

I wandered into the kitchen, still dough-headed from sleep, or lack of sleep, to summon a drink of water from the sink. It came out in a transparent brown stream originating in the bowels of the city. . . . The water had to pass through the most insalubrious regions of the city before it trickled into the sink; it had to pass through pipes laden with lead and caked with rust. I raised the cup to my lips; the water in it smelled bitter; I smelled it. . . . I prepared myself to drink it down. . . . I knew that I should not drink the water, no matter how much I wanted it. . . . There were visible impurities in the water, masses of impurities. . . . Even in the dim light I was able to discern a cloud of impurities in the shape of a flower opening beneath the surface and spreading out, turning slowly, brushing the sides of the cup with phosphorescent streaks. The voice of my familiar spirit told me, there's poison in that water; the water is laden with poison, and disease. . . . The water was quite insalubrious. . . . I poured it down the drain. . . . The insalubrious regions of Minneapolis . . . the river . . .

I went outside and gathered the morning newspaper from the front step and returned to the kitchen, determined to make sense of the newspaper, the opaque, inscrutable newspaper, which is written in an almost impenetrable code. I removed the plastic cover, slipped off the rubber band, unfolded the sections, spread them out on the kitchen table with the front section on top, turned

past a headline that said IT'S A PUPPET GOVERNMENT, past a headline
that said THIS IS STUPID; WHO WROTE THIS?, past a list of THINGS THAT
APPEAR GRAY AT NIGHT, past a list of MY FAILINGS AS A NEWSPAPER, and
started reading. I couldn't concentrate. . . . I could hardly see the
newspaper because it had not been completely imagined. It was like
a newspaper in a movie, where you never see more than the first
page, because only that page has any printed matter on it, because
someone has decided that you don't need to see more than the
outermost layer. In fact, all newspapers are like that. . . . In the one
I was holding there were gaps in the writing, pages were missing,
columns of words were smudged or printed over one another,
words came off on your fingers when you held the pages to turn
them. I could almost see through the pages. . . . The newspaper
is opaque because it is perfectly transparent. . . . The eye plunges
through it with nothing to hold onto. . . . You have to wear special
gloves, frictionless gloves, to hold the newspaper. . . . You have to
wear special glasses to keep the words from blurring. . . .

I was aware of a centipede on the wall at my side. It was
bolting down the wall like a lightning bolt, heading for the floor
or a hole in the wall that I couldn't quite see, a hole that would
probably look too small for something the size of a centipede to
crawl into. . . . The centipede was about the size of my thumb. . . . As
it moved it was tracing a jagged path that would end on the floor,
if it got that far. I immediately understood that I would have to kill
it. Already I was shaping the newspaper into an instrument that
could be used for killing a centipede without touching it with one's
hands, since I didn't want to touch it with my hands. . . . The words
on the outside of the newspaper were coming off on my hands as I
packed the sections of the newspaper into a roll and stood before
the wall where the centipede had stopped moving. Maybe it had
the idea that I would be unlikely to kill it if it wasn't moving . . .
if a centipede can have an idea . . . or maybe it was waiting to see
what I intended to do. It was very close to me but it could not tell
what I was thinking, even though it was right by my head where the
thinking was taking place. Nor could it reach out to protect itself or
climb onto the newspaper, which would have made it difficult for

me to kill it without touching it. Most likely I would have dropped the newspaper then, and the centipede would have gotten away, if it had survived the fall, and I imagine it would have, but its movements were limited to the wall where it had suddenly stopped hurtling toward the floor. Already I regretted what I was about to do. I was not looking at the centipede as a person of science; I saw the centipede as a statement about the house I was living in, that the house was cold, damp, and dark, a cavernlike place where a centipede would like to live. I knew that there were other centipedes inside the walls that did not bother me so much because I didn't see them even though I knew about them. Living in a house with centipedes meant that you occasionally saw a centipede, but they generally kept out of the way. Still, I knew that I would be terribly frightened if I failed to kill the centipede and it escaped into the wall, and if I killed the centipede I would be frightened also. Then I would have to worry about reprisal, payback . . . revenge from the community of centipedes, or if there was a god who looked after centipedes, I might be punished in that way too. Or imprisoned in the body of a centipede . . . It didn't sound so bad, now that I thought about it. . . . It would be reported in the newspaper, only you wouldn't be able to read it there (because of the glare on the surface of the newspaper that prevents you from reading it).

I was not moving, I was thinking about what I might do and what the consequences of my thoughts would be if I carried them out. I was kept from moving by a quantity of thoughts, or it was force of imagination that prevented me, because the thoughts came from that. The centipede was not moving because it had no thoughts; it was not interested in thinking. Eventually the centipede would think so little of me that it would start moving again, but perhaps it would not continue in the direction it had set out on, because the forces that had persuaded it to go in that direction would not impinge upon its awareness as they once had. The centipede would have to start from scratch once its apprehension of me, a thing capable of movement threatening destruction, had faded out of the equation. In this moment, anyway, it was minimally aware of me. . . . It was preparing to react to whatever I was going to do with a sublime lack of preparation, while I was thinking enough thoughts for both of us, because I was also trying to guess what the centipede might do, how it would respond, what it was thinking, which was a fool's game because I wasn't giving it anything to think about. By now I was not really looking at the centipede . . . in fact, I was looking at the newspaper, which had been folded over, exposing a photograph of the baseball player Kirby Puckett who had recently retired. A holiday had been declared in honor of his retirement. . . . His picture had been in the paper for several days running, and I had learned to recognize it by now. . . . His picture in the paper indicated that his batting average, since he had been a designated hitter, was on one of the pages somewhere. . . . I was trying to read the caption below the photograph to see if that was where it was, but I would have had to unfold the newspaper to do that. The picture showed his face, he was smiling graciously, he had on a small fur hat that covered his ears and fastened with a strap under the chin. . . . Then my unsteady gaze, which had been following a line of type that I was trying to decipher, reached the end of the line, and instead of going on to the following line, which was tucked away in a fold, drifted off the page altogether and focused on the space on the wall that the centipede still occupied. I've had that happen to me before. . . . It sometimes happens that I'm staring at the newspaper while around me, in the room where I'm standing, something is in a state of crisis. The newspaper makes absorbing reading because of its apparent difficulty . . . one has the feeling, as one turns the pages of the newspaper, that one is approaching the secret, that one is slowly unveiling, leaf by leaf, what the newspaper conceals.

I wondered if the newspaper could be rolled up too severely for the purpose I had in mind. It had to be solid so that when it struck the centipede it would crush it, but if it was too compact it might only hit part of the centipede, perhaps only an inessential part, or miss it completely, since the centipede would try to get out of the way when it felt the newspaper descending, whereas if the newspaper covered a wider area the centipede would be unable to escape its shadow. I relaxed my grip on the newspaper and let it fan out, slightly, in my hand. The centipede did not strike me as innocuous although it was not moving; it looked vicious to me, and it looked uncomfortably large, although I was much larger. It struck me as unreasonable, since I could not reason with it. I had a feeling like the feeling you get from doing some kinds of machine work: You can start to feel attached to a machine, your movements are part of its movements. . . . This is shown in Fritz Lang's *Metropolis* in an exaggerated form, where the worker who controls the machine does so by embracing it, matching his arms to those of the machine; and in *Modern Times* where Chaplin tries to eat his lunch while his body, still under the spell of the machine it has been working, continues to perform its mechanical task . . . and although I've never done machine work, I've had that feeling with certain machines, that the machine and I are performing a double action enclosed in a single gesture, that the machine is doing what I cause it to do, and the movements of the machine necessarily entail my movements, although I could stop moving at any time, and if I did the machine would continue doing what it was doing until someone did something to shut it down. What had happened to produce this feeling now was that the centipede and I were frozen in a charmed circle in which no possible combination of thoughts could produce even one action, and instinct could not possibly produce any action, and this was so even if all the thoughts and instincts were in the service of possible actions and had action as their goal. The only force that seemed capable of producing any action was some kind of action, which, considering the way things were going, would have to come from another source. Now it seemed absurd to suppose that a thought could end in movement. It would be just as absurd to imagine that you could move things around with the mind alone, by telekinesis. . . . Why, this centipede was situated only a few inches from my head, and I couldn't get it to move no matter how hard I thought about it.

We were attached to one another, the centipede and I, in the way that a machinist is attached to a machine and the parts of a machine are attached to one another, so that if one of us moved in any way, the other one would have been forced to move also.

Even with this strong attachment, which was not merely a physical one since we were not physically attached, we could not hope to arrive at an understanding. I knew what was going to happen and the centipede did not. I knew what was going to happen, it could not be put off for very long or finally prevented by a powerful attachment that was both physical and spiritual, if that is the word for it. It was in a spirit of resignation, almost of defeat, of giving in to a base impulse that I had been struggling against without success, that I struck the wall in the place where the centipede was, as though I had recognized something about myself that I did not like particularly, although on the other hand I was not especially disturbed by it. I did this in a very sloppy way, so that I was struck by the sloppiness of what I was doing as I was doing it. I wished that I had come up with a better plan, because I had thought very hard about what I was going to do but never got around to planning it out in all the time I had spent thinking about it. What happened was that I had not hit the centipede very hard because my arm had been in a bad position when it started to move; it was a little weak besides from maintaining that position during the time when it was not moving. The newspaper must have struck the centipede but not hard enough to do any damage. . . . There was still a mark in the place where the centipede had been: The newspaper had left a dark smudge around it, and the wall had taken some of the color and shape of the centipede. Now the centipede was sweeping across the wall again, looking for a crevice to slip into, and I had to strike it a second time. This time I pressed my hand into the side of the newspaper so that I could feel the body of the centipede giving way under the paper. When I lifted the newspaper there were two marks on the wall, one a faint imprint at about the level of my head, and the other a little lower, where the transparent jelly from inside the centipede was smeared against the wall, and other parts of the centipede, limbs, mandibles, pieces of the antennae, were stuck to it. What was left of the centipede was attached to the newspaper, mainly the outside of it, the head, the body, some of the jelly, and the thin limbs on the outside like a fringe. The limbs continued to wave in the air but were no longer connected to the centipede. . . .

Don't think the question of why the kitchen is empty will be
decided in the kitchen.

Now they were connected to the newspaper. . . . I could see some of the words through them.

28. Non-potable water

I was still holding the newspaper when Hallamore entered the
kitchen, or he may have come in earlier when my face was only
inches away from the centipede. Yes, that's how it happened,
because I didn't notice when he came in, so I must have been in
the middle of killing the centipede then. I didn't know how much
of this he had witnessed and I couldn't tell from his face, which
was shadowed over, what he thought. . . . I had not turned any
lights on in the kitchen. . . . I was a little angry at him, I guess, for
leaning in the doorframe and watching while I deliberated and
finally killed the centipede, because I didn't like the business of
killing centipedes and would have appreciated some help. Also I
was angry because he never did anything to announce his presence,
because if he had I might have behaved differently. I might have
acted more swiftly, not because his presence gave me courage since
he was courageous himself and always looked splendid, but rather
because I felt weak in his presence and afraid of being a coward or
making a mess. I think he knew this and liked to sneak up on me
when he got the chance. Not that he planned it, but he knew that
he had an effect on me and got a thrill out of magnifying it as much
as possible. He was always turning up after I had done something
that I wasn't too proud of, and he never said hello or used my name
or did any of the things that people do to put others at ease, he
never smiled at me although I usually had a very nice smile for him
because I had always looked up to him and wanted him to think
I was all right. I wanted him to think well of me, so I would have
done things differently if I had seen him there, and I would have
put some thought into what I looked like while I was doing them. I
often thought that I was past caring about my appearance to others,
but when I saw him standing there I wondered if my clothes looked
as though I had slept in them, although I wasn't sure whether I had
slept, but it didn't matter as far as the appearance of the clothes was
concerned whether I had fully lost consciousness or not.

What alerted me to his presence was his polite cough.

Hallamore was always coughing. . . . He had caught one of those allegorical diseases that are usually fatal to characters in novels, particularly the novels of Henry James, but the phenomenon is hardly limited to James. Other than the cough, it didn't seem to bother him very much, and the cough didn't seem to bother him very much either. It came at odd moments, and its effect was mainly rhetorical; somehow I always heard it as a comment on what I was doing or thinking. Funny, isn't it? . . . Surely I didn't think that he knew what I was thinking, except I did have that thought once or twice; I really managed to convince myself that Hallamore was reading my mind, and I tried to fill my mind with kind thoughts, intelligent thoughts, and thoughts that weren't too sexy.

"What would you think," I said, "if you saw that I was thinking that you were looking into my thoughts? If you knew that I heard your cough as a comment on my thoughts?"

"I would think you were selfish, obviously," said Hallamore, "selfish enough to imagine that I've been afflicted with this lung condition just so that it can teach you something about yourself that you should know already. Because when you hear my cough, you're hearing my death. This is how I'm going to die, probably."

"That's why I always hear your cough as a rebuke," I said. "Your cough seems to say, 'Willy, you're conceited, you're egotistical, you think that Hallamore has to suffer so that your thoughts can be expressed.'"

"No, don't use that faucet," said Hallamore. "The water that comes out of there is made of centipedes."

"Just to wash my hand?" I said. "It's still encrusted with bits of centipede."

"You'll only get more centipedes on it," said Hallamore. "Transparent centipedes. Linked together. In a stream. Glistening as they emerge from the faucet. With a faint blue tint (they put something in the water to keep it from smelling like centipedes, and that colors it blue)."

29. Unmindful = full of unmind

"If I blindfold you and lead you into the kitchen," said Mercy, "you could be in your own familiar kitchen and not know it."

"The house I live in has no kitchen," I said. "Where have I been? I must have wandered into this house by mistake . . . and there are other people living in this house. . . . What newspaper is this? And the centipede? I murdered a centipede; in a stranger's kitchen I ruined a strange newspaper; I have written a novel in the water that beads on my fingertips, *Arrogance, a novel.*"

"This isn't really a house," said Hallamore. "It's an old vending machine warehouse, converted into apartments by my sister."

"If I blindfold you," said Mercy, "force your mouth open, stuff a sponge in it, and apply a strip of duct tape to your lips; if I hobble your legs, tie your arms behind your back with your wrists joined to your elbows; if I then grasp the hair on top of your head and, pulling on this hair in sudden jerks, direct you into the kitchen, you might discover that your kitchen was a more sharply-defined space than you had previously assumed."

"If she tells you to go with her," said Hallamore, "don't go with her."

"I'll go with you, but I don't know why I'm going," I said. "I don't know what makes me go. Something makes me (although I'm aware of not really wanting to)."

"If I blindfold you and herd you into my kitchen," said Mercy, "we might be able to determine, at last, what you're made of."

"Whatever stuff a person is made of," said Hallamore, "a person is made at least partly with ideas. But I'm a person who hasn't had an idea in a long time. That's okay, something can be made with something without finally having any."

"When they made me, they left out the ideas," I said. "They had no idea what they were making."

"If I break a glass jar over your head," said Mercy, "you might discover the fully-equipped kitchen of your dreams."

"A curtain descends over the theater of consciousness," I said, "covering the eyes to protect sleep (as though sleep could leak out through my eyes) . . . or to protect the mind from light (as though light could enter my mind)."

"Struck down on the way to take his biology exam," said Hallamore. "All his ideas went into the jar and were preserved."

"How did this get in here?" said Mercy. "Have you been eating in the kitchen again?"

"Why are you so disturbed by the concept of food in the kitchen?" said Hallamore.

"Did you eat this?" said Mercy.

"No, that looks like the impression from someone else's mouth," said Hallamore. "See, the dents don't correspond to the placement of my teeth? Let's try your mouth. . . ."

"The date on the wrapper doesn't prove anything," said Mercy. "It doesn't tell you who ate a thing that isn't there."

"How can you tell something was there if I ate it?" said Hallamore.

"How can you tell that you have chosen the wrong restaurant?" said Mercy. "At some point you begin to understand that the restaurant was wrong (but you will never admit that you were wrong)."

"You ate it, and you continue to think about it," said Hallamore. "Your mind is still heating the leftovers in its saucepan."

"You seem to know a great deal about an event that you can have no direct access to," said Mercy. "I mean, if I ate something that existed only in my mind."

"Even you know at least one thing that is quite beyond your experience," said Hallamore. "For a moment, your consciousness is swallowed up in a larger consciousness."

30. The head seen from behind

"Something chased it out of my head," I said.

"He still doesn't have ideas," said Mercy. "In fact, he seems to have fewer and fewer."

"I'm sorry," I said. "I apologize at the drop of a hat."

"'The drop of a hat': what hat?" said Mercy. "He doesn't wear a hat. He doesn't even own one!"

"If you give me something to eat," I said, "I might recover my idea. Everything depends on food."

"Fewer and fewer ideas," said Hallamore, "until his only idea is 'lunch.'"

"My ideas are getting worse," I said, "sometimes I have to eat lunch twice."

"Take your hat off so I can see the dent I made," said Mercy.

"That's where my ideas came out," I said, "when Mercy let my brain out of its doghouse."

"Your head is closer to an unfilled doughnut than an abandoned doghouse," said Mercy.

"The interior of your hat is lined with something soft, like fur," said Hallamore. "And there's a tear in the lining."

"I'm tracing a line in the dust that gathers inside your hat," said Mercy. "This is the background against which you think."

"Better put it on your head," said Hallamore, "before your mind collects more dust."

"Ah, it hurts my head!" I said. "It feels like shouting in my ear!"

"Oh Willy, your hat printed a word on the back of your head!" said Mercy. "The word is GRIMACE, no, it's only the smashed body of a centipede, but it looks like a grimace, unless you're seeing a word printed on your eye, or the shadow of a centipede crawling over your eye."

"You shouldn't have repaired the lining of your hat with newspaper," said Hallamore. "Have you ever seen Mercy do her performance? That would dull the pain resulting from more direct forms of contact."

"But the newspaper already gives me a dull pain," I said.

"We had to invent an artist for tax purposes," said Hallamore. "So she invented herself as the 'artist of the head.' Hey Mercy, do your 'head art' for Willy."

"Want to see me perform?" said Mercy.

"'Head art'? I don't know," I said. "It sounds a little . . . sort of . . . intellectual."

"Well, my art is not for public consumption," said Mercy. "If that's what you mean."

"Trust me, it's very brainy," said Hallamore.

"That would be a rather crude application of my art," said Mercy. "Still, if you insist . . ."

"Conceptual art? It's not my cup of tea," I said.

"Tea?" said Mercy. "You've never seen a cup of tea in your entire life!"

"I'll make the tea," said Hallamore.

"Not for me, thanks," said Mercy. "You don't know how."

"Objects that produce this condition," said Hallamore. "Let's see . . . does tea heighten awareness? Does the newspaper?"

"He doesn't put water in it," said Mercy. "He doesn't know how tea is made."

"The problem of making tea without getting centipedes in it is a tricky one," said Hallamore, "which, to be totally honest, I haven't quite solved."

"Conceptual tea? That's all we're likely to get," I said. "They must be very resourceful to get anything out of this kitchen!"

He doesn't put water on it. He doesn't know how tea is made.

31. As though all the molasses had been concentrated into a
    smudge on the glass . . .

"Are they living on invisible molasses?" I said. "Traces of molasses?
Essence of m.? Because there's no other food in the apartment."

"The closest thing to food in Mercy's apartment," said
Hallamore, "the only thing resembling food, is this jar of molasses
which appears to be empty—no, not empty, because it contains two
centipedes . . . as though someone poured out the molasses, and
the drops that remained at the bottom hardened and turned into
centipedes."

"Because they look like living molasses," I said. "Their bodies
are shiny and dark from eating molasses . . . and they move so
slowly, curving with the glass (faster, though, than molasses usually
goes) . . . and they adhere to the glass and leave sticky marks behind
them . . . and all over the room and in the hall, on the floor . . . and
on the walls and the ceiling."

"As though all the molasses had gone into them," said
Hallamore. "As though they had discovered a transparent layer of
molasses at the bottom of the jar, a thin film no one saw, but they
could feel it under their feet, and they shared it with one another,
and in that way prolonged their existence . . . as though glued to
the bottom of the jar by the molasses that lured them in, and if they
ever got their legs free of the stuff they only sank back into it, too
exhausted to climb the sides . . . "

"Those are tassels, not centipedes," said Mercy. "I collect
them from men's shoes . . . men I know. How do I get them? With
my teeth."

"Not all men's shoes have tassels," said Hallamore. "Most of
them don't. . . ."

"Those," said Mercy, "are the ones I've already harvested."

"Mine, for instance, do not," I said.

"I got yours a long time ago," said Mercy. "They're in one of
these jars somewhere. . . ."

"Surely one can't live only on shoelaces," I said. "Centipedes,

I suppose, if she caught enough of them and prepared them creatively, she could make a pretty decent meal out of."

"Tea leaves arranged in a triangle around a cup of water," said Mercy. "Tea leaves in a watertight jar submerged in a bowl of water. I see my brother has been here."

"No one likes the bitter tang that centipedes leave behind when they pass through your mouth," said Hallamore. "Some people dilute it with milk to kill the aftertaste. But that isn't enough to prevent them from forming a nasty, indigestible ball in your stomach."

"He leaves these attempts at tea all over the apartment," said Mercy. "Teabag submerged in vinegar. Teabag taped to the outside of a jar that may once have contained molasses (the lid of the jar is labeled IMAGINARY MOLASSES). Teabag submerged in coffee. What are you doing?"

"Oh, I forget, does coffee have centipedes in it too?" said Hallamore. "Back to the drawing board . . ."

"Here's that book he didn't like," said Mercy. "He hides things that he doesn't want to see, and I keep finding them in unlikely places. Here's a postcard from your sister. . . . Oh, and here's a letter (where are all my tassels?)."

"This tea is not good enough," I said. "Try again."

"That teapot, with pages from the newspaper submerged in water, is actually a trap for centipedes," said Hallamore. "I wasn't trying to make tea in it."

"I'll make the tea," said Mercy. "He still hasn't figured out how to do it. He doesn't even know the difference between coffee and tea (a significant difference!)."

"I can use that postcard from Natasha," said Hallamore. "I've invented a machine for converting memory into tea."

"Nothing's coming out," I said.

"It only works with childhood memories," said Hallamore.

THE VENDING MACHINE SONG

I like coffee
I like tea

I'm Jimmy Jingle
The vending machine king!

Give me a jingle
A swallow will tell you
And the color of the tea
Will be green!

Fill bowl fill
Heal bowl heal
And the color of the tea
Will be black!

I'm the slippers man
I've got cakes and tea
I bring the winter
To Minneapolis!

I'm the autocrat
Of coffee and tea
I'm Jimmy Jingle
The vending machine king!

"It hums, it sings, it releases tea, coffee, and chocolate from its reservoir in a transparent brown stream," I said. "How do you know that it isn't alive?"

"I'm a Coke can!" said Hallamore.

"You're a human being!" said Mercy.

"I'm a Coke can!" said Hallamore.

"You're my little brother, you have a paper route," said Mercy. "I'm allowing you to stay in my apartment only until you've paid off your college debt."

"I'm a Coke can!" said Hallamore. "The next stage in the gradual improvement of sensual enjoyment."

"Willy, did you want tea, coffee, or chocolate?" said Mercy.

"Or did you really want something else?"

"I have to make a decision," I said. "Before my failure becomes my decision."

"Unable to decide between tea and chocolate?" said Mercy. "Why not have both?"

32. Tea or masturbation (difficult choice)

"Sofa cushions stained with tea," I said. "Carpet stained with tea. I see your brother has been sitting here."

"You've got to stop drinking tea on the sofa," said Mercy. "And in bed."

"I don't know how many cups of tea I've spilled on that sofa," said Hallamore.

HOSPITAL CORNERS SONG

How can you love me if I don't love myself
How can you love me if others don't love me
How can you love me if you still love me
If you still love me why won't you talk to me
If you still love me why do you want to make me
    uncomfortable
If you still love me how can you love me

"What a picture of incredible waste," I said.

"He's always forgetting tea," said Mercy. "He leaves those jars of experimental tea steeping all over the place, and I keep finding them. He gets involved in something else while waiting for them to magically turn into tea and just forgets about them."

"Sheets stained with tea," I said. "Shirt stained with tea. More of your brother's leavings?"

"Yes, he leaves them out until he knocks them over," said Mercy. "He races around in an attempt to organize his new scheme for making tea, and accidentally spills and scatters the remains of his old schemes wherever they happen to be lying. Or he hides them if they offend his sight, and I end up sitting on them or knocking them over. Drinking endless cups of tea, passing bottomless cups of tea through his body, he passes from one life into another, from the living room into the bathroom and back again, like the horse that carries on its back what it will eat; passes into and out of the

100

living room, or passes out in the living room, on the sofa, with a warm cup of tea resting in his lap so that when he shifts in his sleep it will soak him and wake him. As soon as he lifts it he sees how he's going to break it, sees exactly how it will happen, sees that the accident might be prevented if he took a little more care, but he does nothing to stop himself, put the jar down, get a better grip on it, with two hands. And he puts far too much effort into lifting the jar, maybe because it still looks bigger to him than it is, and ends up flinging it against the wall, smashing the jar and spilling molasses on everything—a molasses Chernobyl. I can't take any more of this."

"This tea is making you too emotional," said Hallamore.

"Are you sure it's the tea?" I said.

"He has no self-control," said Mercy. "He doesn't even wait until I've left the house before he starts drinking tea again. Sometimes I think he wants me to be aware of precisely how much tea he consumes. Once I caught him drinking tea on my bed, and when he looked up and saw me it gave him a start and he dumped tea all over himself and on my quilt. Another time I went into my room and he was just sitting there flocculating!"

"Pulling floccules out of his sweater?" I said. "Sweating floccules? Imitating a floccule?"

"More like sprinkling tea over the blankets," said Mercy. "Dotting them with blobs of tea . . . wetting and pulling apart the little pills . . . and all the time I'm waiting for him to leave the house so that I can masturbate."

CINNAMON TOAST SONG ("The Lost Girl")

It's bad luck to get run over by a truck
It's bad luck to get knifed in the street
It's bad luck to lose all your money

It's bad luck to have an incurable disease
It's bad luck to get addicted to crack
It's bad luck to desire children

Aaron Kunin

It's bad luck to be a person
Shut up in a bag and stolen
Devoured by mice crushed

Under a giant hand or run over
By thousands of children on bicycles
Like illustrations

In the old *New Yorker* the frying pan says alas
Alas and no help comes
I push my cart in the street

I wonder why they run over you
And what you want with that long shallow box
They are imprisoned half the year in stoves

With soft white draperies they dare not
Peep out for the cold darling I swear
I do not understand what is the matter in
   Minneapolis

"I'm ready for my tea now!" said Hallamore.

"Here's another cup of tea for you to knock over," said Mercy. "And here's some coffee for you to drink. . . . Oh, and here's the newspaper."

"I like coffee, I like tea," said Hallamore. "She brings me coffee, she brings me tea . . ."

"And chocolate!" said Mercy.

"Who cares about chocolate?" said Hallamore.

"She serves you tea as though it were an insult," I said.

"It is an insult!" said Hallamore. "It's too thick!"

"I put some sludge in it," said Mercy. "To weigh it down. So you won't spill it."

I push my cart in the street.

WORDS SONG

Ball bearings pencils eyeballs gruel
I hope you like gravy!

"There's something wrong with the bread you're serving," I said. "I can't write anything on it; it doesn't retain an impression. And it's rose-colored; it makes my hand somewhat pink."

"We received this bread in the mail," said Mercy, "sent to us by some people living in New Haven. But the package was not large enough to contain the long thin loaf in its entirety, so they had to tear off the ends. Now all that's left is crumbs. Put your hands in the package, fill them with crumbs, shovel them into your mouth. This is the food of the dead, the stale bread that they eat. It took a long time to get here because, unfortunately, they also got the address wrong."

"This reminds me of the army!" said Hallamore.

"You, my friend, have spilled your last cup of tea," said Mercy. "Your new wife will cure you of staining your shirt."

"Resolved," said Hallamore. "Never again to drink tea on the sofa. To spill no more cups of tea on the sofa."

"Somehow you always miss the end of the tea," said Mercy. "The end happens while your mind is elsewhere . . . 'occupied' with something else."

"I'm going to keep drinking tea until I get an idea," I said. "Until something other than tea occupies my thoughts."

"Why stop then?" said Mercy. "The machine gives you a free porcelain animal after fifty cups."

"If I keep drinking past the point of inspiration, my idea might drown in so much tea," I said.

33. The artist of the head puts her head together in order to see

"Doesn't it bother you," I said, "that everything in your living room comes out of a machine?"

"Everything in this room causes a feeling of disgust," said Mercy, "so let's talk about unpleasantness in the arts. Can I take your plate, Willy?"

"Typical," said Hallamore. "She discerns the only interesting thing in the room and wants to remove it."

"I didn't do anything," said Mercy. "I looked at it and felt that I approved of it."

"When I heard you say my name, I felt shy," I said, "as though caught in a shameful act."

"You've made an art of self-loathing," said Mercy. "What I learned from you is that the part of yourself you're most ashamed of is interesting and can be turned into art."

"The warm plate resting on my knees is the most interesting thing about me," I said. "I was going to present it to my biology teacher in memory of my lunch."

"What most interests me about you is what you're ashamed of," said Mercy. "No one else would have chosen it as a thing to be ashamed of; it's interesting and should be cultivated."

"What am I ashamed of?" I said. "Why is it considered degrading to take the chemical in its pure form rather than drowning it in a medium?"

"Your self-loathing art is creating a medium for bacteria to grow in," said Mercy. "Your novels put girls to sleep, but my art puts them to work."

"Lack of interest becomes interest in the same way that money combines with money," said Hallamore. "The novel creates interest by pretending not to care: Suddenly it becomes interesting and may be worth a lot."

"The novel isn't interested in you," said Mercy. "You have pretensions toward art."

"My artistic pretensions are my art," said Hallamore.

"I have an announcement to make," said Mercy. "Hallamore is still fighting World War I, by sea and by air. Willy is still fighting the Napoleonic Wars (on the side of the British)."

"Mercy is militant," said Hallamore. "She's still fighting the French Revolution (on the side of the Terror)."

"Why do you encounter everything as a model you can imitate until you no longer encounter anything?" said Mercy. "My excellent friends, you have despised art!"

"We revere art and artists," said Hallamore.

"Hallamore," said Mercy, "you have despised literature!"

"We adore literature," said Hallamore.

"Natasha," said Mercy, "you have despised pastry!"

"We are martyrs to pastry," I said.

"Willy," said Mercy, "you have despised sympathy!"

"We are very sympathetic," I said.

"Your fine professions are a mask for your contempt," said Mercy. "And now, because you have been a very disrespectful audience, I will present 'Experimental Theater Piece Number Five' by Adrienne Rich. What's great about her plays is the sense they convey that incredible suffering is taking place and you're powerless to prevent it."

MERCY SONG

Here is something to see
And here is something to see it with
And I'm telling my tale
And I'm crossing the stage
And the stage is behind me
And the stage rises before me

Returning to Minneapolis at age sixteen
I found myself unable to describe the things I was
    seeing

And this is the place where I hesitated
And I see it again
And I can't make up my mind
It was like the interruption of a journey or its
    continuation
Or the continuation of an interruption

"I interrupt you," said Hallamore.

And I continue talking
We made a decision to postpone the decision
And then we arrived at a decision

"Or you might obtain the same result by another method," said Hallamore. "Using different processes."

And then we arrived at a result
And then we arrived at a house
House surrounded by trees
House surrounded by time
House threatened by clouds

Returning to Minneapolis at age sixteen
I found myself unable to describe the things I was
    seeing

"This is where she installs her head," said Hallamore. "The artist of the head teaches the curatorial staff to fabricate a head for her use."

"She pauses, caught between her desire to perform and her desire to observe," I said. "Torn between what she's doing and what she's seeing, equally pleased by both, she doesn't know where to look: at her rapt audience? Or at herself?"

"Once you are onstage, you no longer have a moment to watch," said Hallamore.

And this is the house where I couldn't make up
  my mind
House threatened by clouds
And I want to enter this scene

"It's the easiest thing, entering a house," said Hallamore.

And this is the door I entered by
And this door will slide shut with a sucking sound

Returning to Minneapolis at age sixteen
I found myself unable to describe the things I was
  seeing

And I could not keep from going up another
  flight of stairs
And somehow I lost my footing
And I put out my hand to catch myself
And I could not keep from falling

The theater of my actions is fallen
Do you forgive my ideas
Do you forgive me for my ideas
What else do you forgive me for

"Boring," said Hallamore.
"Your head art is too intellectual for me," I said.
"I don't get it," said Hallamore.
"I kind of spaced out at the end," I said.
"I was looking in the mirror on the wall behind you," said
Hallamore. "This mirror shows another room. Then it's more like
a window. And the shadow in the corner—"
"That's not a poet's shadow!" said Mercy.
"Oh, I thought it was a diagram of your head!" I said. "We
organize these events either to celebrate or humiliate the artist
(sometimes we don't know until the event takes place), or, in some

Provoking "involuntary physical response"; therefore, pornographic.

cases, to bore ourselves silly."

"The artist shyly manipulates two groups of paper dolls," said Hallamore. "In group A, the dolls are relaxing and reading, picnicking, coupling. In group B, they are violently folding, unfolding, and tearing each other, turning one another into chairs, reading matter, food. I have never seen hands move so fast; I almost can't see them. 'The end of this story does not look like the beginning.' 'My publisher urged me not to show it.' 'An obscene story.'"

"The artist shyly holds aloft a can, allowing each one of us to inspect what he is holding, to ascertain that it is indeed a Coke can," said Mercy, "regards it skeptically (is it really a Coke can?), then blows into its opening as though whispering a part of the lecture that only this can can bear to hear."

"A stripe of sweat blooms on his upper lip," said Hallamore. "The shame-artist is smoking two cigarettes, so that he can keep one of them in his mouth while he shakes off the ash that collects at the end of the other into a convenient receptacle. For this purpose he uses two empty Coke cans, dividing his attention equally between them so that no one can tell which one he prefers. He is also drinking from another Coke can, although he sometimes stops himself just before putting it to his mouth, as though uncertain that it really is a Coke can, afraid, perhaps, that he has chosen the wrong one, afraid that he won't be able to put it down or that once he starts drinking he won't be able to stop."

"A bloom of sweat stripes his upper lip," said Mercy. "He talks faster and faster as he goes on. Soon you can hardly make out the words."

"Four Coke cans at the corners of the podium," I said. "Between them: two books. The shame-artist, behind the podium, gesticulating madly, as though trying to measure the distance between himself and the cans, his hands darting out and veering away suddenly just before making contact, unable to decide which one of them he wants to pick up, unable to remember which one has Coke in it, how much Coke is in there, and which one is empty. Does he want a drink of Coke? Does he want a mouthful of cigarette ash? Does he want to pick up the empty can? Or does he want to pick up one of the books?"

"Keep your hands in your pockets!" said Hallamore. "Or you might knock over one of those cans! (I almost feel like knocking them over myself!)"

34. Hallamore at the moment of victory

"What are you going to do?" I said.

"If I told you, you would stop me," said Hallamore. "What are you going to do?"

"I'm going to stop you from telling me," I said. "Don't tell me what you're going to do!"

"If I don't tell you," said Hallamore, "I might not do it."

"Do what?" said Mercy.

"If I told you that, if I told you, you would stop me," said Hallamore, "what would you do then?"

"Huh? I'm not sure," said Mercy. "I wouldn't stop you."

"You never listen," said Hallamore.

"The artist collapses, as though struck by an invisible can of molasses," I said. "He feels as though someone asked him a question, and there is only one possible answer. He waits to see if there is something else in his head—"

"But there isn't," said Hallamore, "so why not go ahead and say what you were thinking in the first place?"

"This takes such a long time," I said, "that he appears to be working very hard to come up with an answer."

"You hit Saul Bellow with a Coke can?!" said Mercy.

"I wasn't aiming for his head," said Hallamore. "And besides, Willy threw the green end of a strawberry at him."

"I wasn't throwing a strawberry at him," I said. "I was waving to him and the wave encountered a strawberry."

"I did it (threw the can at him) because I loved him," said Hallamore. "He looked thirsty. . . ."

35. Hallamore in the act of throwing a Coke can at Saul Bellow

"I did it to destroy my feeling of triumph," said Hallamore. "I created it specifically to deface what I had created."

"Aren't you afraid that the can will retain an impression of your grip?" I said.

"I'm afraid it might retain an impression of the artist's head," said Hallamore. "It's not immediately visible, you have to find it."

"Brought out of your can, you're free to spoil," I said. "Thus serving as a reminder of what you really are underneath."

"My can has no dent," said Hallamore. "I'm indestructible!"

"You're a human being!" said Mercy.

"I'm an evolved Coke can!" said Hallamore. "All the molasses ran out of him and went into me—an infusion of transcendental molasses!"

"Excuse me, I think you mean 'transcendent'?" I said. "I'm working on an article on molasses."

"I'm teaching a class on molasses," said Hallamore.

"I wrote my thesis on it," said Mercy. "Here's my diploma from the Northrop Collegiate School: INTELLIGENT MOLASSES."

"How can you tell that it's intelligent?" I said. "Because it's sour? How intelligent is it?"

"I've invented a machine for measuring the intelligence of molasses," said Hallamore. "My diploma is from the Dunwoody Institute of Technology."

"This diploma case is empty," I said.

"Well, they kicked me out last week," said Hallamore. "But they're going to allow me to participate in the commencement exercises anyway."

36. Literary outcasts
   (for Lee Woolman)

"I don't consider myself an outcast from literature," said Hallamore, "but I have been kicked out of some schools. First they kicked me out of the Do Your Own Thing Baby School. Then they threw me out of the Black Leather and Chains School."

"That's a good school," said Mercy.

"Personally," I said, "I don't consider myself an outcast from literature, but I did fail my orals."

"Was that at the I'm Looking For An Answer School?" said Mercy.

"No," I said. "That was at the Hey Man How Are You Doing School. You should try it if you want an education designed to produce unreadable novels (not 'bad,' just unreadable)."

"I don't consider myself a literary person," said Mercy, "but I am Jewish."

"I call myself a Jew," I said, "but I don't observe the Sabbath, the high holidays, or the dietary restrictions; I don't read Hebrew; and none of my friends is Jewish."

"I don't consider myself an outcast from Judaism," said Hallamore, "but I did get kicked out of Hebrew school."

"I don't consider myself an outcast from literature," I said, "but Reynolds Price says that I'm uncommercial."

"I hardly think that I'm an outcast from literature," said Mercy, "but Gordon Lish rejected my manuscript."

"I don't," said Hallamore, "consider myself an outcast from literature, but my play has been rejected several times. I took it to the Guthrie Theater and they rejected it flat out. Erin McGonagle rejected it. 'I ABSOLUTELY reject that,' she said."

"She thinks she is an arts administrator," said Mercy. "She thinks she controls the flow of art in Minneapolis. She doesn't realize that there is no art in Minneapolis."

"What does it mean," I said, "to be a literary outcast? If the newspaper hates my novel and reviews it savagely, if it takes my

Is the snake immune to its own poison?

novel in its teeth, latches onto it, and worries it until it expires, does that mean that I have been expelled from literature? If so, how can I still be literary?"

"To be rejected by literature," said Hallamore, "is one way of being recognized by literature, in the same way that you have to approach Erin McGonagle if you want to encounter her disdain: Every separation from her that she enforces can only bind you to her for as long as she pushes you away. Being rejected by the newspaper (which does not recognize literature) makes you a different kind of outcast: an outcast because you are literary. Like the Jews."

"Hallamore buys a movie ticket," said Mercy. "He thinks he is a patron of the arts; he is a fashion plate . . . or thinks he is . . ."

"I didn't even know there was opera in Minneapolis," I said, "and meanwhile Hallamore has been to one by Rameau."

"I'm surprised you didn't read about it in the newspaper," said Hallamore. "The newspaper does not recognize art; nor does it recognize art-singing; but probably it would be interested to learn that there are a few singers in Minneapolis who have classical training and are able to pronounce the libretto (which is adapted from Racine!), and it would also want to know who paid for it, where the money came from and how much was involved."

"The expenses for putting on a French opera in Minneapolis are surely prohibitive," said Mercy. "Possibly Hallamore had something to do with it; he tends to have a hand in those pockets. He has a real knack for putting money into art or putting together enough money to make art. He may have played the *continuo* part on the harpsichord (but who provided the harpsichord?) as well."

"Could be," I said. "I forgot that he has a degree in music from someplace in Chicago. He could have sung one of the parts, Hippolyte, maybe. He has a pretty good voice, you know, and sings baritone and counter-tenor, or at least he can imitate a trained singer, which he sometimes does as a joke, and that is probably as close to the real thing as you are going to get in this city."

"If someone doesn't help me with this," said Hallamore, "I'm going to be late for the opera."

"There's a tax on bowties in Minneapolis," said Mercy, "or a tariff in case you have transported something like a bowtie or the materials for making one into the city, but the materials for making bowties are hard to find no matter where you are. This makes it difficult to create some kinds of art."

"What's the problem with this bowtie?" said Hallamore. "It keeps suggesting that the choices we've made as a culture are wrong."

"Maybe the purpose of the bowtie is to be crooked," I said. "How do we know that it wants to be straight?"

"This is a special bowtie," said Mercy. "One that castrates."

"This bowtie is sublime," said Hallamore, "perched on the edge of a cliff."

"This bowtie is perfect, everyone should throw their neckties away," I said.

"And there you are," said Mercy. "A terrible bowtie is born."

"It is such a pleasure to watch Hallamore lose his hair," I said. "One almost wills it to happen. Even as one reassures him: 'A trick of the light.' 'Perfectly normal.' 'No change.'"

"To Minneapolis," said Hallamore, "an opera such as *Hippolyte et Aricie* must seem like a transfusion of the wrong blood type, because it's a dangerous and possibly fatal operation for the city, but not, I don't think, for art."

"Which is the outcast?" I said. "The blood, which suffers the rejection? The patient, whose stability is threatened by the introduction of a foreign agent?"

"It must be Minneapolis," said Hallamore, "because you can't be an outcast and be literary at the same time."

"You mean, of course," said Mercy, "that you can't be literary and in Minneapolis at the same time. Just being in Minneapolis automatically excludes you from literature. It's like a state of diplomatic immunity: When you're in Minneapolis, nothing literary can touch you."

"Can you have an immunity to literature?" I said. "Is Hallamore immune to literature?"

"Is the snake immune to its own poison?" said Hallamore.

"I'm terrified of literature," said Mercy. "Everything I do

is against literature, an attempt to expel it from my speech, my thought, my heart, my sphere."

"We are all literary outcasts," said Hallamore, "writing at three removes from literature. I write non-literature, Willy writes pseudo-non-literature, Mercy writes anti-literature . . . and the newspaper writes toothless anti-literature."

"Leaving only Erin McGonagle to write literature," said Mercy. "I guess that makes her the outcast."

"I'm not a very literary outcast after all," I said, "but I do have the same initials as Alfred Kazin."

"I hate anything that isn't literature," said Hallamore, "but I wouldn't say that I love literature."

"I think of myself as a woman," said Mercy, "although I share many traits with some men."

"I don't think of myself as a woman," I said, "but you and I have a lot in common."

37. It doesn't interest him

"Literature doesn't interest me," said Hallamore.

"Literature must be talked about," said Mercy, "but only one or two things can be said about it that aren't misguided and boring."

"Still," I said, "that's better than not talking about it."

38. The mandarin

"Let's wake him up," said Mercy, "and make his life interesting on the way home, okay?"

"You made me promise," said Hallamore, "to keep you away from his house in the unpleasant hours of the morning. You told me not to drive you there, and if you suggested it, I was to reject it, to plead with you to remember your better intentions, to distract you, and not to trust you. His house, you said, was a mistake you wanted to avoid."

"I retract, I abjure," said Mercy. "Suddenly I have an awful yen for him. It's dormant for a long time, and the smallest signal will set it off. A letter is enough to set it off, if he sends me one—or if he doesn't. It's all out of proportion. It's not really a thing I take pleasure in."

"I made a solemn promise," said Hallamore.

"Break it," said Mercy.

"The telephone is ringing," I said. "Hello, hello?"

"Let's go to Savran's!" said Mercy. "Okay? Won't you come with us to Savran's?"

"I don't think they sell coffee there," I said.

"Who said anything about coffee?" said Mercy.

"As usual," I said, "I blame myself for something that is partly your fault."

"Yes, you are programmed correctly," said Mercy.

"Don't call again," I said.

Malvern House threatened by clouds.

39. A thought cut out of the mind

"Cut it out of your mind," said Hallamore. "And hold it in your hand."

"I have to see him," said Mercy, "if only to recover what I saw when I didn't care about him. Everyone says he's changed."

"I can't tell if you want me to talk you out of it," said Hallamore, "or are you proud of losing control and betraying yourself, and do you want me to betray you and not control you?"

"There's something about him," said Mercy. "No, there's nothing particularly special about him, nothing that could inspire a strong attachment, nothing that could justify it. When I see him, he isn't nearly as splendid as I think he's going to be, but he sets me off anyway. What kind of mind works in this way? Gets stuck on things like this? With no outward provocation?"

"What kind of person has such a mind?" said Hallamore.

"I'd better try again," said Mercy.

"The phone rings," I said. "A knife descends from the sky and cuts me in two. Yes, what is it?"

"Yes, this is Natasha speaking," said Mercy.

"Oh ho," I said. "Are you talking in your sleep?"

"You always cover part of what you say with a laugh," said Mercy. "Are you laughing because you expect me to laugh? Are you suggesting that I should be laughing too?"

"A sentence disintegrates in a laugh," said Hallamore. "And his body seems to collapse. He folds in half."

"It's something I don't think much about," I said, "and I also try not to talk about it, but in your case I'll make an exception, because you seem to have good motives."

"Are you laughing at your own loss of control?" said Mercy. "What are you laughing at?"

"I'm laughing because you're not laughing," I said. "I'm laughing to keep from talking. If I laugh at it I won't say it, and if I don't say it, it won't happen."

"I'm laughing at you," said Mercy, "because I don't

understand you."

"When you laugh at my jokes, you belong to me," I said. "Your thoughts are saturated with my outlook."

"When I laugh, I am helpless," said Mercy. "But when you fail to realize the implications of your own jokes, or when you realize them too late, when you realize them after you say them and start to laugh when you hear me laughing at you, then my laughter possesses you, then I show you an aspect of your outlook that you didn't know existed."

"I feel slightly worse," I said, "as a result of talking about myself. I always feel sort of—I am searching for the exact word—diminished after talking about myself at any length, as though I have become a baby again. The words lose their magic when I say them, as though nothing that comes out of me could point back at me."

"Why do you pull so hard?" said Mercy.

"What if the phone doesn't hang up?" I said.

"Are you hanging up on me again?" said Mercy.

"I'm hanging up on myself!" I said.

"Aren't you going to congratulate me," said Mercy, "on my respectful behavior toward Willy?"

"If virtue could be rewarded," said Hallamore, "wouldn't that make it a commodity? Like coffee?"

"What is it about coffee?" said Mercy. "It must be an obsession peculiar to men."

"You call me, telephone," I said, "and I am ready to serve you. You ring, and I answer—hello, hello?"

40. Who is speaking when literature speaks?

"Why should the telephone have a book?" said Mercy. "Even the telephone has a book, why not you?"

"Telephone," I said, "how are you able to speak with Mercy's voice? Did you learn that trick in your book?"

"Why do you close your eyes when you open your mouth," said Mercy, "when you talk, when you eat, when you sleep?"

"I'm closing my eyes because I don't want to see what I'm saying," I said, "because I'm lying, because what I see contradicts what I'm about to say. Because I'm in pain, because I'm ashamed of what I'm about to say and I don't want to see how you're going to receive it. Because I don't want anything that I release from my mouth to come back in through my eyes."

"Are you going into your 'Clever Hans' routine again?" said Mercy. "How much is three and five, Clever Hans? How much is three and five, Johnny?"

"When he can't remember something," said Hallamore, "he stamps until it comes to him. It sounds like the end of intermission at a play: 'Please take your seats, ladies and gentlemen; the play is about to begin!'"

"You ask the same questions every time," I said. "I tell the same stories, you always seem mildly interested, but you don't retain anything. What are you doing to me?"

"I'm making fun of you, Willy!" said Mercy. "I'm imitating you!"

"You don't know me well enough to make fun of me," I said. "In fact, I love it when you make fun of me, because it only shows how little you understand me."

"I know you well enough to telephone you," said Mercy. "So I can make fun of you even if I don't understand you."

"Your way of making fun of me doesn't touch me," I said. "Nothing you say touches me. I accuse you of not knowing anything about me, failing to remember what you used to know, not being really interested in me, not even pretending to be interested, not bothering to work yourself into a state of artificial interest. You can't make fun of me."

"I can make fun of you even if you don't exist," said Mercy. "I can make fun of something that doesn't exist."

"You've become a Board of Welfare for me," I said. "You control my thoughts by making it impossible for me to think of anything else."

"I must learn to content myself with proximity," said Mercy. "To become indispensable . . . until there's no difference between the contents of our heads, yours and mine."

"Being inside a person's head is not the same as knowing a person," said Hallamore. "It's not even a way of knowing."

"I hate the way you behave in restaurants," I said. "And on the phone. You stand in front of everything I want to look at, and your voice intrudes in every conversation, until I start to answer you in your own voice and wonder who is speaking when I speak."

"Who is speaking?" said Mercy. "What voice do I hear? When you open your mouth, who speaks?"

"The telephone is speaking to you," I said. "The novel is speaking to you. Literature is speaking to you—through the telephone. I feel about you the same way I feel about the police or the FBI or a collection agency. It seems that your feelings about me are strictly juridical, which means that they aren't exactly feelings anymore."

"I'm sorry, you're breaking up," said Mercy. "You say you want to talk to Hallamore?"

"No, I just talked to him earlier today," I said, "and it had a poisonous effect on my consciousness. All my perceptions were poisoned."

41. Contact a poison control center immediately!

"I wish I had a formula to control the mind," said Mercy. "My own mind, I mean—or anyone's."

"Formula to control the mind," said Hallamore. "'I can't control it!'"

"I can't control what he's thinking," said Mercy. "I can't even control what I'm thinking. Every idea that motivates me, no matter how clever, is capable of being replaced, through a mysterious process of regression, by one of my bad old ideas, as though the mind were a machine for reproducing an emotion."

"You yearn for the company of young novelists," said Hallamore. "You imagine yourself falling into his arms when you arrive and he opens the door: Oh diabolical young novelist, I must have you!"

"Oh inept young novelist," said Mercy, "what have you wrought? Oh melancholy young novelist, what weighs down your novel? What makes it tilt to and fro? What makes it shimmy and sway? What makes it burn? How can we set it right?"

"You call me, telephone," I said, "and I reply. I want to hold you, to reassure you. I support you with my own hand. Your voice brings me back to life, which isn't necessarily something I wanted to be brought back to."

"You call me 'telephone,'" said Mercy. "Your name for me."

126

You don't know me well enough to make fun of me.

42. When the telephone rings, it is always a surprise

"The phone doesn't want to be put down," I said. "This pleasure doesn't want to be put down."

"Who wants to be put down?" said Mercy.

"A baby crying wants to be put down," I said. "Antaeus wants to be put down, when Herakles is holding him in the air, squeezing life out of him."

"I have looked over the things you sent," said Mercy. "I don't understand them."

"I can't remember," I said, "what things I sent or why I sent them. I'm fairly certain that I sent them to her, although I can't figure out how I did it since I don't have an address for her. I don't know how to find her but the materials I don't want her to see have a way of finding her, or she has a way of finding them."

"I have a trick," said Mercy, "of finding out things that you want to keep from me."

"He read over the letters carefully before sending them," said Hallamore, "to make sure he had not inadvertently made a confession."

"Could he refer to such a thing without intending to?" said Mercy.

"He felt that it would be possible," said Hallamore. "He might blurt out his secret without noticing, because for him his secret was such an ordinary thing that he saw every day. Because she wasn't used to it, it would stick out to her."

"But if she had no inkling," I said, "no sign of it could be visible to her."

"There was a lot in it that she wouldn't be able to understand," said Hallamore. "She didn't have the background. She couldn't understand what the letters referred to, but she would know what they meant in reference to him and her: that he was keeping something from her and was having trouble keeping it from her, that it was getting away from him and seeking her out."

"He washes the dishes for me," said Mercy, "he pays the bills,

128

he takes care of the kids . . . I don't understand it."

"He read it over again and sent it," said Hallamore. "He committed it to memory and sent it. He sent it out and could not remember what was in it."

"I wanted to call it back," I said. "I returned to the mailbox, wanting it back, knowing that it was too late: The mail had been picked up already. Nonetheless, I returned to the mailbox and put my arm inside as far as it would go and caught at things, hoping that it had somehow returned, hoping that it was still in there, that the envelope had not fallen into the bin, perhaps, that it had instead rested somewhere inside the lid, in a niche where it could still be retrieved . . . and what if it had? What if someone had already retrieved it?"

"He had put his name on some papers," said Hallamore. "Papers that were, to say the least, incriminating. A recent photograph of him, not a very flattering one, was included among the papers. It was too perfect."

"It was like releasing a helium balloon," I said. "Mailing it was like watching it rise and vanish into the heights."

"He wondered if it would be returned for insufficient postage," said Hallamore.

"I wanted to put myself in the *Dunciad*," I said. "I wanted to write the *Dunciad* again so that I could be in it. Teach me how to write, Carole Maso, so that I can put myself in the *Dunciad* . . . so that I'll find my name there when I open the book. . . ."

"He addressed her as though she were the author of the *Dunciad*," said Hallamore.

"She may teach you how to write," said Mercy, "or she may not, but you will end up in the *Dunciad* whether you want to or not."

43. Around the house and in the yard

"The radiator sounds as though it is typing a letter," I said. "The refrigerator sounds as though it has been dropped down a mineshaft. The telephone rests on its hook—"

"Even the telephone has a hook," said Mercy. "Why not you?"

"I rest on my own hook," I said. "I hang myself up. . . . How easy it is, in the middle of winter, to write a novel in Minneapolis! Especially after a good meal in a huge restaurant. In the cold everything seems sawed-off and foreshortened, including my fingers. A pen cannot be made to write; the tines of a fork break off against the white of an egg; and the eye will not see very far. The distant horizon, the immense buildings in the clouds, the clouds passing overhead, shuffling, crossing, and disappearing behind one another, look rather obviously like a scrim lowered only a few inches in front of me. I am afraid, almost, to look up from my work and brush my nose against a cloud."

"For as long as I've known you," said Mercy, "you have suffered from a basic inability to relax, to rest on your hook."

"A piece of paper is blowing in the snow," I said. "It passes noiselessly over the snow and makes shadows in footprints. And all of my old friends are far below me. My friends—how much I like them! The people I like—how much I like them! I feel strangely tempted to let them in. . . ."

"From here I can see the upper part of your room," said Mercy, "part of the ceiling, bookshelves lining the walls, and the upper part of your body floating and turning around like an eel's body."

"Seeing you through this window is like falling through a window," I said. "I'm closing my eyes so I don't see you, so I can't read what you want me to say from your forehead. It was painted on your forehead in red letters, so I looked away. . . . I looked at the floor: It was in the floorboards. I looked at the ceiling: It was in the ceiling tiles, so I closed my eyes."

"You could still see it," said Mercy. "Because what you saw wasn't in any of those places."

"It was in you," I said.

"No. Not in me," said Mercy. "In you."

"No?" I said. "What did you want me to say?"

"I don't know, but that wasn't it," said Mercy. "What ceiling tile did you read that off of?"

"I'm closing my eyes," I said, "so that I can pretend that I'm talking to someone else."

"I'm sorry, Willy!" said Hallamore. "I tried to keep her away from your house in the unpleasant hours of the morning."

"'Unpleasant' for whom?" I said.

"I made a promise knowing that I could not keep it," said Hallamore. "I promised something I didn't have. I deliberately placed myself in a situation where I was expected to do something, and I knew I couldn't."

"Is that a crown you're wearing?" said Mercy.

"If I were king," said Hallamore, "I wouldn't wear a crown."

"How would you know that you were a king?" said Mercy. "What else makes a king? The throne?"

"If I were a conductor, I wouldn't use a baton," said Hallamore. "If I were a policeman, I wouldn't carry a gun or a baton. If I were a soldier, I wouldn't wear a uniform."

"Don't you want everyone to know that you're a soldier?" said Mercy.

"I don't like to think that anyone thinks well of me," said Hallamore, "or better than I think of myself. I must dissuade them from their good opinions. I have somehow inadvertently put on a good front when I abhor putting on a good front."

"Perhaps I am mistaken," said Mercy. "I really believe that if you want something, you can have it. But it isn't a question of wanting it, how much you want it, or how often you think about it. Also, it isn't a question of personal qualifications, credentials, merits; whether or not you deserve it—no. Nor is it a question of strategy. It's only a question of ASKING FOR IT."

"When I saw you," I said, "you were standing where I'm

standing now, by this window, bleeding from the top of your head to your chin, shaking bits of glass and leaves out of your hair, and you had on a green dress that I've never seen you wear since then."

"Remember that dress?" said Hallamore. "She used to wear it all the time. It must have gotten ripped up going out the window."

"I tore my dress," said Mercy, "coming back through the same window. A mistake I could easily have avoided by walking around the house and entering by the door."

"Some of us were wondering how he could be so cruel," I said. "Some of us were wondering what she had done to make him do that to her. 'Hallamore is gentleness itself,' I heard someone say, 'why would he want to push his sister through a second-floor window?'"

"I thought it would be amusing," said Hallamore. "I didn't mean to push her so hard. It was a mistake."

"I wanted her to look at me," I said, "the way she looked at him when she emerged from the window. And I could also see that this was what she might look like when she got older."

"I felt as though I had just returned to a place that I had known well as a child," said Mercy. "How often had I fallen out of that same window? None of this was unfamiliar, and yet none of it had lost its ability to surprise. Already I was on my feet again; already I was extricating myself from the tree into which I had fallen too quickly to determine which branches were unsafe and which were sturdy enough to support my weight; already my hand was starting to swell—some of the fingers had gotten a little mangled from being dragged over the windowsill in an effort to stop my fall with no suede glove to protect them, because I had removed the glove, I think, to check my watch."

"I didn't see it happen," I said. "Suddenly she was in the room, a woman with leaves in her hair, standing ragged and torn in front of the broken window, apparently furious, looking as though the window itself had stepped out of its frame and was slowly shattering in our midst. I now believe that she was standing absolutely still, but she seemed to be quivering because so much detritus was falling away from her, pieces of glass and wood and paint from the

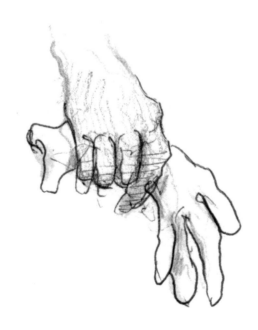

Seeing you through this window is like falling through a window.

window—and blood was pouring down the magnificent stem of her neck."

"I stepped over the sill," said Mercy, "shredding my favorite dress and knocking the rest of the glass out of the frame, and it spilled over me, creating another unbelievably awful cut in the side of my head, and I congratulated myself on my self-possession. Too soon!"

"They were married, and I was bewildered," I said. "He would not have treated his wife like that. I didn't know him well enough to know that he had no wife; sometimes you have to see the biology teacher to divine the actual relation between a brother and sister, because nothing else connects them. Now I ask myself how I could tell that they were connected at all, what they shared that caused me to postulate, wrongly, that they were married. Is it possible that I entered into this relation desiring to share in their existence?— No. Even then I knew it was closed to me."

"As I re-entered the room, spitting glass," said Mercy, "I had a premonition of a mistake. I saw it coming but could not rouse myself to avert it; I could see what shape it would have but did not know what it would look like; I still do not know. I trusted my brother to look after me, but that might not have been a mistake; that might have prevented the real mistake if only I hadn't returned. Is it possible that I entered this room desiring to share in this existence?"

"She approaches with one arm outstretched," I said, "not in a threatening manner, but with a friendly look on her face, even turning her head up to show off her smiling mouth which is a little like a slotted spoon, apparently intending to shake his hand, but instead battering the side of his head with an umbrella that has suddenly materialized in front of her, an umbrella that just a moment ago didn't even appear to be anywhere near her, and as long as she's done it once, she may as well do it repeatedly, until someone drags her away and pries it out of her hands. I wanted to be one of those people who held onto her arms and pulled her away, but felt that that was not possible, it would not be right for me to take advantage of the situation like that, although I was already taking advantage of it by enjoying it from where I was standing; and I also knew that I was not strong enough, that if I had put my hand on her shoulder she would have knocked me down, still smiling faintly, as though brushing a stray hair from her jacket—which, to be honest, I would not have minded especially and might even have enjoyed."

"My friends," said Mercy. "I depended on them to protect me, to help me to avoid mistakes and keep me from looking bad. They failed me every time. After a while the mistakes would be obvious to me, but by then it would be much too late to do anything to prevent them. My teachers were supposed to save me from mistakes; instead they led me into mistakes. Only Natasha kept me from mistakes."

"Her friends led her down the back stairs and into the kitchen," I said. "I looked over at Hallamore and thought that he was a glum-looking fellow. That was the phrase that came to me; I imagined myself saying it to someone, describing this scene, shaping it. And then I imagined someone else using the same words to describe me."

"What a mess, what a disaster, what a failure!" said Mercy. "What good was there in walking on two legs if it was going to come to this? Down the stairs, legs! (How often I had fallen on these stairs! How little I understood about this house! And how was I supposed to understand all the things that went on in a house when I knew so little about what went on in my own body? Everything it did was a response to something in my mind—and what did I know about that?) Onward, legs; down the stairs, two at a time!"

"The most difficult thing about going into a kitchen," said Hallamore, "is learning the system. No one else can explain it because they are probably not aware of it; they developed it so that they would be able to cook and eat in this environment without noticing one another (or the environment)."

"No mistakes are possible here," said Mercy. "When I look back on it, I see that I did nothing wrong. It's obvious to me now that my fall from the window was not a real fall; it was only a confusion fall. The confusion was not a mistake; its purpose was to keep me from being mistaken, but unfortunately it prevented me from recognizing the mistake when it happened. The mistake was you. Everyone else was looking after me; everything else conspired to force me out. You were my mistake, and you didn't mean anything to me; you were only a piece of furniture to me, and you turned out to be radioactive."

"Everyone has a system," said Hallamore. "Every house: a system. Anything is a system if you say it is."

44. Is this a system?
(for Sarah Jane Lapp)

"Look at this book," said Mercy. "Someone has underlined in it with a thick black line. Rather messily too. It seems that the purpose of the line is to obliterate the words and not to emphasize them."

"Look at this book," I said. "It doesn't open. Someone has driven a nail through it and nailed it to another book—what other book I can't say, because its cover is entirely obscured by the first one."

"Look at this book," said Mercy. "It's glowing. The words are on fire, but not the paper."

"I can't look at this book," said Hallamore. "It glares at me. It's terrifying."

"This book burned my hand when I picked it up," I said. "I dropped it, and the sound it made hitting the floor gave me a sharp pain behind my eyes and in my forehead. It was like a new understanding of how the head is put together, and how much wasted space there is in there, because there were quite large pockets of emptiness where the pain seemed to end."

"Don't look at this book," said Mercy. "I've hardly glanced at it, and my eyes are on fire—even now, they are brimming with these useless tears."

"This book gives off a greenish light," said Hallamore. "But the light is too faint for you to make out the words in the book."

"A sickening vapor emanates from the pages of this book," said Mercy, "inflaming the eyes and making them itch terrifically, but you must resist the temptation to rub them, because that will only make it worse."

"Look at this," I said. "I cut my thumb holding the corner of this page to turn it. The skin seems to disintegrate around the wound, which extends much farther down than I realized at first, almost to the base of my thumb."

"Look at this book," said Hallamore. "I can't tell if there are any words in it. The ink is exactly the same color as the paper."

"This book sighs when you open it," said Mercy. "You can feel it on your hand—a warm breath of decaying matter."

"I feel as though I've been dipped in boiling water," said Hallamore. "I'm like a book with the cover ripped off and the title page ripped out."

"So I get this strange object in the mail," said Mercy. "It's invisible, but it feels like a book. When I look at it, it's like I'm studying the lines that cross my hand, which supports it."

"Look at this book," said Hallamore. "The pages are mirrored so that you can see only yourself in them."

"You can't look at this book," I said, "because you're inside it, on the other side of the page."

"Look at this book," said Mercy. "I don't understand it. It's in some foreign language I can't identify."

"Put it under your pillow when you go to bed," said Hallamore, "and see if it creates a vivid and continuous dream in your mind."

"Look at this," I said. "This is new. I was holding this book when they told me Valla was dead. My thumb was marking a certain page, and it still bears the impression. The page that my thumb was marking turned red, and the page that my index finger was marking turned yellow, and the pages between them showed an incremental progression to black. And when I removed my hand, it was the same as before."

"When you look at this book," said Hallamore, "you're only seeing a small part of it, because it exists in many copies."

"All these books smell like glue," said Mercy, "and the pages are curling up at the edges."

"Look at this one," said Hallamore. "The pages are falling out."

"John Ruskin," I said, "*Sesame and Lilies*."

"A book of lectures," said Mercy. "It smells musty; it's about . . . beauty. But I wonder what kind of beauty is supposed to reside in these brittle, dark-yellow pages, which are no longer attached to the spine?"

"This book is coming apart in small flakes," I said, "so that you can't pick it up without getting a lot of it on your hand. How can it have anything to say about beauty?"

"But it is a beautiful book nonetheless," said Hallamore, "and, despite its condition, a repository of the beauty that it wants to preserve as a king's treasure (and which it is slowly destroying as it decays)."

"This book is telling me to smash the windows," I said. "The windows are telling me to toss the book out the window."

"This book is worthless," said Mercy. "Cast it into the fire, therefore."

"This book has neither dramatic tension nor psychological depth," said Hallamore. "Burn it."

"*Sesame and Lilies*," I said, "out the window. We no longer need or want any text."

"Satisfactory. And why you're throwing the novel out the window?" said Mercy.

"To bring it down to my level," I said. "To confirm your low opinion of me."

"My not-so-high opinion of you," said Mercy, "doesn't require independent confirmation. Why are you throwing the novel out the window?"

"To see if it would kill someone from this height," I said. "To illustrate the death of serious literature."

"That is such a good answer," said Mercy, "that I almost believe you. What part of this defenestration did you not intend?"

"I intended the outcome but not the action," I said. "I intended the failure."

"Then you have succeeded," said Mercy, "if failure isn't always 'failure to succeed.' Why are you throwing the novel out the window?"

"To avoid throwing myself out the window," I said. "It was either the novel or myself."

"Smash!" said Hallamore. "Another book goes through the window."

"Trollope," I said, "*Barchester Towers*."

"A novel," said Hallamore, "not a piece of sculpture."

"A novel," said Mercy, "not a field guide to wildflowers."

"A novel," said Hallamore, "not an explosive device concealed in a novel."

"A novel not to be used to prop open any door," said Mercy.

I've hardly glanced at it, and my eyes are on fire—even now,
they are brimming with these useless tears.

45. He leans back and asks if she has read his play yet

"Did you get a chance to read my play?" I said.

"I didn't know you had written one," said Hallamore. "How come you didn't show it to me?"

"I have a few specific criticisms about one of the characters," said Mercy. "Snide, arch, glib, he plods along into one insurmountable problem after another (at times the problems seem to come out of nowhere), with lots of misfortunes that never seem to stifle his spirit, and he is almost asking for them and stumbles into them when so many could have been avoided. He's always going, being thrown out of this joint and admitted into this one. He never initiates any action, he only responds to what the others are doing. I like his being an artist of sorts—dabbles in dance, visual arts, poetry, so on—as well as having aspirations to becoming a teacher. What he needs is to channel all that antic energy into a more manageable project. . . ."

"This is not what he needs to hear," said Hallamore.

"It isn't finished yet," I said. "So far it consists of a couple of scenes and this prop: a menu that has some laminated pieces of food (egg, sandwich, doughnut) stuck to it."

"I've never seen anything like it," said Hallamore. "If you put this much attention to detail into other aspects of the play, I feel that you can only succeed."

"It's not badly written—for a soldier," said Mercy. "Well done, soldier. Good writing."

46. She falls asleep and her dream walks into the room

Perhaps I have laid it on a little thick. I remember everything perfectly, perhaps more perfectly than things were. It's hard to be clear. "It never rains but it pours," I said. "There is something profoundly right about this mindless remark. Anyway—"

I knocked on the door.

"I'm asleep," said Natasha. "Do you want to take the T.V.?"

"No," I said.

"You can take it if you want."

"No, thanks."

47. She falls asleep and her dream walks into the room (2)

Hallamore knocked on the door.

"Whom do you seek?" said the door.

"Natasha!" said Hallamore.

"It's on the dresser," said Natasha.

"There's no one here," said the door. "Natasha has awakened. Rejoice!"

Hallamore beat his head against the door.

"No need to beat yourself against the door," said the door. "Rejoice: Natasha has awakened."

"No need to hold a funeral for the sleeping," said the T.V. set.

48. His undiminished appetite (for food)

"Did photography create all these images only to leave them idle?" said Mercy. "No! The stars and planets are not idle. The sea is in constant motion; the earth likewise. You lazy girl, don't you know that hard work conquers everything?"

"Natasha, we have bagels!" said Hallamore. "In a brown paper bag! From Gelpe's!"

"Did you hear that?" said Mercy. "Hallamore says he has two thousand four hundred bagels."

"Look what I have in my bag," said Hallamore. "More bags. In my first bag, I have bagles—"

"Ah, bagels," said Mercy, "everything in the world you could ever want."

"—in my second bag," said Hallamore, "I have coffee—"

"Ah, the sacred and profane mystery of coffee!" said Mercy. "Have Hallamore bring his coffee in bowls, barrels, craters; let Hallamore pour his coffee into cups; let Hallamore splash the trees with coffee, so that even the trees will have coffee; let Hallamore cover Natasha's desk with coffee, and therein write NATASHA. Spill coffee across Natasha's desk—gush! I LOVE YOU—pour coffee into Natasha's lap. Pour some into a saucer, and let Natasha's cat have a taste, and even the cat will have coffee (who now pushes herself against my foot, as though my foot will feed her)."

"—in my third bag," said Hallamore, "I have a sink—"

"Yes, good. Animals want to rent videos," said Mercy. "Just like people want to rent videos. Even the kitchen sink wants video-colored food."

"—in my fourth bag, I have a cat—"

"Your cat, Natasha," said Mercy. "Your cat, Thisbe, a very hungry cat, a very confused cat, who pushes her face against Hallamore's bag, as though that will feed her."

"—in my fifth bag—"

"Oh, you have a trustee's hat," said Mercy. "Is that a trustee's hat?"

"Yeah, I stole it from a trustee," said Hallamore. "I saw a trustee walking by, and I kind of snatched it off her head. In my sixth bag—"

"Excuse me, bagel is spelled b-a-g-e-l," I said. "And no explanation was provided for the sink."

"The kitchen sink is a thing," said Mercy, "that shows what we mean by 'paternalistic.' Oh Hallamore, with this symbol of America, this thing of greatness, you have outdone yourself."

"In my sixth bag, I have a centipede—"

"The ghost of the dead centipede that Willy murdered in my kitchen!" said Mercy. "It looks like a frown or another expression of pain or worry, and it makes a sound like the bell in a high school that recalls all your troubles, and when you run your hand along its back it feels really . . . just awful, but you can't keep yourself from stroking it and increasing your anxiety, and sometimes it comes to life and runs across your hand and makes your skin crawl. And when you don't see it the entire room becomes charged with discomfort, because you don't know where it went or out of what crevice it will elect to return."

"—in my seventh bag—"

"The magic number seven, which we all love!" said Mercy.

"I don't seem to have anything in the seventh bag," said Hallamore. "Perhaps it is the bag itself. A person could wear it on her head, like a hat."

"Don't count on it," I said.

"And you, Hallamore, are a turd of a person," said Mercy. "You are like the camel that sticks its head in the tent, and before we know it, the camel has defecated all over the tent; and your bags are so much brown paper, that hold only air."

"The essence of being a poet," said Hallamore, "is screwing around and being sleepy all the time."

"But you're not sleepy all the time," said Mercy. "You never sleep."

"I can't sleep," said Hallamore. "I've eaten too much. I went past the sleeping point."

"You don't even want to be sleepy!" said Mercy. "You collard, you're a disgrace to the profession."

49. Siesta

I opened the door.

"Can you see anything?" said Mercy, as though she were far away.

"Toenail clippings in Natasha's red carpet," said Hallamore. "Christmas cactus perched on the T.V. set. Dust-ruffle running along the edge of the bed. Chessboard leaning against the window. Arm of the T.V. set rusted pink."

"Would you like a piece of gum?" said the T.V. set.

"You always offer me gum, but I never see you chewing any," said the red carpet. "If you don't like gum, why do you buy it?"

"I like gum," said the T.V. set. "I just don't chew it; I swallow it."

"Cookies are coming," said the dust-ruffle.

"Bagels are coming," said the toenail clippings.

"Cookies are kissing," said the Christmas cactus.

"My hand is colored silver from being put in front of the T.V.," said Hallamore. "Silver is a quality of light. I have to touch my hand to the screen just to convince myself."

"Mind if I smoke?" said the T.V. set.

"Go ahead," said the dust-ruffle.

"Rats! Out of cigarettes," said the T.V. set. "Cigarettes. Remind me to buy some more."

"You always run out of cigarettes," said the red carpet, "but I can never catch you smoking. Where do they go, I wonder?"

"I don't smoke them; I swallow them," said the T.V. set. "But wait. Surely I am mistaken. Surely this is not our brother Flavio."

"Surely not," said the red carpet. "Hey, ho, Flavio!"

"You must have a wrong person," said the Christmas cactus. "Flavio! I thought you'd never come."

"Have you met Aunt Tillie, Flavio?" said the dust-ruffle. "Here, meet Aunt Mildred."

"Give us a kiss," said the toenail clippings. "How you've grown since you went away."

"Who's your little friend?" said the T.V. set. "Surely not Hallamore."

"His name is Hallamore," said the dust-ruffle, "and he eats them raw."

"Oh no, it is Hallamore," said the red carpet. "Hey, ho, Hallamore. Remember the night Hallamore ate all the salmon patties?"

"He ate everything in sight," said the toenail clippings. "Ho, hum, Hallamore."

"Go home, Hallamore!" said the Christmas cactus.

"Hey, watch where you're going, Hallamore!" said the T.V. set.

"Sorry," said Hallamore.

"What's that? What happened?" said Mercy. "Is somebody down there?"

"I just spilled the coffee, that's all," said Hallamore. "I didn't see the desk here."

"Oh! It's coffee," said Mercy. "I thought it was a body!"

"The coffee smells so good," I said. "But I must not have any."

"Let us salute our long-lost brother," said the T.V. set. "Pull up a chair, Flavio, and tell us where you've been."

"I always had a soft spot for you," said the Christmas cactus. "It's been lonely for me here since Natasha kicked you out."

"Sit in a chair," said the red carpet, "and tell us your adventures."

"No one tells stories as well as Flavio," said the dust-ruffle.

"Speak, Flavio," said the toenail clippings. "We never go anywhere. What is the world like?"

"You are thought not to wear pants, Flavio," said the Christmas cactus. "Do you wear skirts? You are thought to wear your hair in ringlets; do you?"

"What's the matter with Flavio?" said the red carpet. "He used to tell much better stories."

"Cat got your tongue?" said the T.V. set. "What's with Flavio? Did he lay the egg that Hallamore hatched? Frère Flavio, why don't you speak?"

the staplers

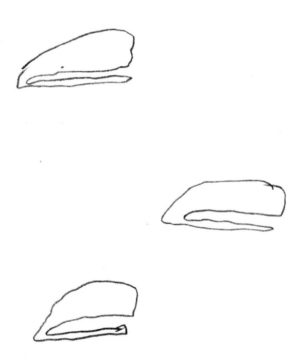

It all happens on a molecular level.

"Him?" said Mercy. "He talks worse than anyone I know. He has no gestures; he washes his hands constantly, like a paranoid English teacher. 'They're all against me. I didn't get tenure. *Why?!'*"

"I am hungry for speech," said the dust-ruffle. "My hunger for speech is such that you could hold it in your hand. My hunger for speech is such that you could test it for doneness with a toothpick."

"You are our newspaper, Flavio," said the toenail clippings. "Please be our newspaper. We stand before you in an attitude of submission that somehow fails to negate your essential passivity."

"I love to hear Flavio's voice," said the T.V. set. "It's just like *Waverly*, listening to him."

"You always talk about literature," said the red carpet. "But, funny thing, I never see you open a book. How do you manage it?"

"*Waverly* is actually the only novel I've read," said the T.V. set. "Mostly I don't read them; I swallow them. Perhaps our brother would like a glass of wine."

"Pressed by hand, Flavio," said the red carpet, "between the pages of a book."

"Great wine, Flavio," said the Christmas cactus.

"Yeah, not from concentrate," said the dust-ruffle.

"You keep calling me Flavio," I said. "But I'm not Flavio. Why do you keep calling me that? My name is William."

"Look at my face," said Hallamore, "reflected in this pool of coffee. It's distorted. It winks at me as it catches the light of the T.V. This is a side of myself I haven't seen before."

50. Kitchen sink realism

"In trying to put his hand on something," said the T.V. set, "he pushes it away. . . ."

"He breaks something," said the dust-ruffle, "by putting his hand on it. . . ."

"He makes it worse when he writes it down," said the toenail clippings. "He hunches over when he sits up. . . ."

"His motive in writing about it," said the Christmas cactus, "was to beautify it."

"I'm not alone in this room," I said. "Am I alone in thinking that I'm alone in this room?"

"It gets worse when he writes about it," said Mercy. "It gets worse, but not because of the writing, not because of the writing but because of him. He was writing about it and therefore failed to prevent it."

"She says obvious things so slowly that they seem profound," said the toenail clippings. "She says them so many times that they gradually achieve a certain profundity."

"I thought it wasn't worth listening to," I said, "because she said it only once."

"Her lack of interest excited him," said the red carpet. "Her disinterest interested him. It happened on a molecular level."

"It all happens on a molecular level," I said. "Everything happens on a molecular level—everything that matters."

"Can't we talk about something else instead of molecules?" said Mercy.

"There's nothing else to talk about," I said. "Nothing else matters. The rest is just a façade, a crust of stuff."

"I like him," said Hallamore, "I just wish he'd talk about something else. He doesn't know the first thing about brain chemistry, but he insists that everything else is just a façade."

"Even the kitchen sink is just a lot of molecules," I said. "To say anything else about it would be absurd."

"My face appears at the bottom of the sink," said Hallamore.

"It appears to rise to the surface when I stand over it, then to drain out when I step away. The In-Sink-Erator does not retain an image, but the mind does. The thing in your mind is the same every time you open it up."

"An event," I said. "A molecular event. One molecule salutes another. The same thing happens in the In-Sink-Erator that happens in your mind."

"Hallamore doesn't talk like other people from Minneapolis," said the dust-ruffle.

"His accent? It is a complete affectation," said the Christmas cactus. "He's just a big softie."

"I think I need another siesta," I said.

"Your siesta is over," said Mercy, "when you start to wonder when the word 'siesta' entered the language."

"My body shows no sign of change," I said.

"His body was changing every day," said the T.V. set. "The sound of his own voice surprised him. A light installed in his stomach began to flicker."

"His feet," said the red carpet, "installed in their clear, high boots . . ."

"Feathers grew out of his arms in tracts," said the T.V. set, "and fell out, leaving a trail of feathers behind him."

"I thought that I was past caring about my physical appearance," I said, "until my physical appearance did something to prove me wrong."

"He puts his name on everything," said the T.V. set. "His name makes it worse."

"It pains him to see his name," said the red carpet. "It hurts his hand to write it."

"My dream is generally the same," I said. "I awaken and believe that someone is in the room with me. Someone is sitting in the chair by the window; I can hear him turning around in my chair, which is too small for him. The blind rattles against the window frame, as it has been doing all night, and he puts out a hand to stop it. What can I do? I must leap out of bed and run away while he is grappling with the blind. But this is almost impossible, because I

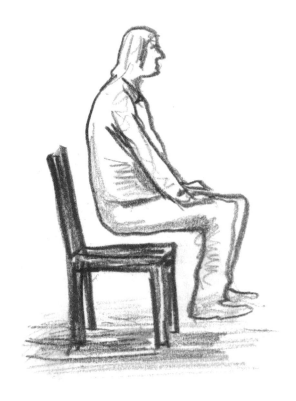

Lucifer/St. Peter.

can already feel his hand resting on my foot: It is going to happen, it is happening, it has happened. Or he is only looking at my foot with a look that I can feel, or he has placed his hand on the bed in a way that picks out my foot through the sheet, the blanket, and the comforter, and pins it down. I still haven't opened my eyes. I shift slightly, as an experiment, and feel something else shifting above me and locking into place. And I am unable to move because I won't let myself move and because he won't let me, because he is holding me down, because he has found a new indentation in my body, a slender inpouching into which you could nail nails or screw screws. I feel his breath in my ear. I yell: 'St. Peter!'; his tongue licks loose circles in my auricle; 'It's you, St. Peter!' I yell."

"St. Peter values our foolish way of thinking and talking," said the toenail clippings.

"St. Peter is made of stone," said the red carpet, "that moves."

51. Lucifer/ St. Peter

"Your biology teachers didn't know about fucking," said the T.V. set. "They did it in the armpit; that's why its hair grew.

"Then Jesus Christ looked down from heaven. 'Why don't they bear children? You'd better go down and see what's the matter, Peter,' he told his servant. Thus St. Peter came to earth and met the biology teachers. 'What are you doing?' he said. 'We're not doing anything special,' they said. 'Okay, just go on doing what you were doing before I got here,' he told them. They started to do it using the armpit. 'Not there,' said St. Peter. 'Here, down below.' He showed them. 'This is it, here,' he said.

"St. Peter ascended to heaven. But he was not allowed back into heaven then. Jesus Christ got angry. 'You have to go back down and live in Minneapolis,' he said. 'You had better go back down and watch over them.'"

"Brother Flavio, I wonder why you haven't committed any sins," said the red carpet. "Is it because you don't know how? Because St. Peter didn't demonstrate it for you? He has to live in Minneapolis because of the way he taught your biology teachers. He feels ashamed and disgusted with himself. He thinks it's an outrage that he has to suffer so that you could have a modern sex education class."

"If you don't sin, they punish you anyway," said the toenail clippings. "If you don't drink the wine, they punish you for not drinking the wine. If you say you didn't commit any sins, they make you take part of the punishment for sins committed by someone else."

"Then it isn't really punishment, is it?" said the red carpet. "It doesn't reform, it doesn't deter . . ."

"Why don't you sin?" said the Christmas cactus. "Were you careless; did you lose something? Did you cut off your right hand to keep from stealing? Or did you cut off your left hand to keep from masturbating? Why not cut off both your hands (but what will you use to cut off the second hand)?"

155

Aaron Kunin

"Don't fight the enemy, Flavio," said the toenail clippings. "Grab hold of him and change him into something like you."

"Some of the men in Minneapolis will commit murder," said the dust-ruffle. "Others will commit rape. Don't you think you should do your share by having some wine?"

"Drinking the wine will keep the crime rate down," said the toenail clippings. "Plus, if you don't drink the wine, they make you drink piss."

"St. Peter hates excess," said the Christmas cactus.

"St. Peter hates deficiency," said the dust-ruffle.

"Are we normal?" said the toenail clippings. "Have we sinned equally?"

"Is it normal to want to be normal?" said the red carpet. "What if I don't want what I'm supposed to want?"

"They ask if they are normal," said the T.V. set, "as though the answer could be no. As though they could be abnormal. As though they had done something that no one had tried to do before."

"Original! Disturbing!" said the red carpet. "Powerful! Oh, thou art the swallower of literature!"

"Come out!" said Mercy. "Come out of the bedroom, Willy."

"Come away!" said the T.V. set. "Come away, foul, foolish, feathery Flavio. Come down from your high tower and go into the bower. Look down where Natasha lies."

"Her body lies like a heap of wheat, under the covers of the bed," said the red carpet. "Her body lies like a stack of pillows in the shape of a sleeping body, there where she lies."

"Her eyes are stars; the stars are her eyes," said the toenail clippings. "She peers at you through chinks in her eyelids. You come at her while she pretends to be sleeping."

"She sleeps with her mouth closed," said the red carpet. "Her lips are so red, they are the color of blood in snow."

"Her hair is so yellow, it is the color of urine in snow," said the dust-ruffle.

"No, no," said the Christmas cactus. "Her hair is brown, so brown it is the color of tree bark in snow."

"Her sheets are so white, they are the color of snow," said the

156

red carpet.

"Who's the most beautiful girl in the world?" said the toenail clippings. "Everyone says: 'Hey, it's Natasha!'"

"Drunk, you are unable to pronounce her name," said the T.V. set. "Nasha. Fisha. Tanaza. Tanasha. Tanasha. Tanasha."

"She must be a goddess," said the toenail clippings.

"Oh, most certainly," said the Christmas cactus.

"A brown pear," said the dust-ruffle.

"Natasha is oranges," said the T.V. set, "bananas, sugar cane, mangoes, seedless green grapes . . ."

"You always talk about fruits," said the red carpet. "How come I never see you eating any?"

"I don't eat them; I smoke them," said the T.V. set.

"Before the firing squad," said the red carpet, "he chews and swallows his last cigarette: *messieurs-dames, les chapeaux!*"

"Why did Natasha kick you out, Flavio?" said the Christmas cactus. "Because you didn't like her cooking? Because you didn't like her friends?"

"I didn't like the cat either," I said. "Or her furniture."

"Because she doesn't love you," said the red carpet. "Why won't she talk to you anymore?"

"I don't know," I said. "Because she read one of my novels."

"Because she doesn't love you," said the Christmas cactus.

"Love brings you down, and it's sick," said the dust-ruffle. "This is the way it is everywhere."

"You are a really fascinating, and really sick, novelist," said the T.V. set. "You are so fascinating you grew feathers. Hey, you're a swan."

"He turned into a swan, because Natasha doesn't love him," said the red carpet. "He was sick with love."

"He wrote her all those beautiful novels," said the T.V. set, "and she still wouldn't sleep with him."

"You must have lived with Natasha at some point in your life," said the dust-ruffle, "if she really is your sister. You must have spent a lot of time with her then, perhaps even slept in the same room, perhaps, on occasion, in the same bed even . . ."

"Could you have forgotten that she is your sister?" said the red carpet. "Surely it is the idea that she is your sister that is the delusion."

"Or do you have two sisters?" said the toenail clippings. "Maybe so—you could easily have as many as two, or possibly three, sisters."

"Back in Cloquet, the town where I grew up," said Hallamore, "there was only one biology teacher, and we had to use outdated books. And here you have two biology teachers all to yourself."

52. Let's shut down for a moment

"We define ourselves," I said, "by the things we do, as my biology teacher used to say. It's a funny thing about language. Start running, and you slowly become a runner; run away, and you become a runaway. Does it really happen like that? A runner runs, a biology teacher teaches biology, an accountant takes a certain account of things? No, no, my other biology teacher would say, we define ourselves by our accessories: Someone who knows how to use a pencil might be a novelist, a dog is anyone who wears a leash, and someone who has feathers is probably a swan. On the other hand, someone who carries a piece of chalk might be a biology teacher, or she might want to play hopscotch; and someone who carries a grand piano might be a concert pianist, or a truck, or a tornado. Sometimes it's hard to tell. What do you think? Did either of my biology teachers actually say any of these things?"

"Probably not," said Mercy.

"But who's to say?" I said. "Who are the objects, after all? Who are the sleeping? Who are the lunatics?"

"Who are the perverts?" said Hallamore. "And who are the animals? Who are the dinosaurs? Who are the lawyers? Who are the barbarians? Who are the robots?"

"Do not make an ape of me," said Mercy, "or I will make a monkey out of you."

"Your biology teacher wears army boots," said Hallamore.

"Your biology teacher had sex with a camel," said Mercy.

"Your biology teacher had sex with a crocodile," said Hallamore.

"The big swan comes at her while she pretends to be asleep," said the red carpet. "She doesn't care. She doesn't know enough to care. If the swan is there for her to respond to . . . she shrugs her shoulders. She doesn't get it."

"It must be hard for him," said the T.V. set. "It must be like rolling in salt. (After all, she is his sister.) Natasha has been sleeping for a long time; perhaps she will appreciate the change. For her,

159

variety is the spice. But for him, it must be as though she is covered in a layer of salt."

"Permanence and change, smack, smack," said the Christmas cactus. "These are the pleasures of being raped by a swan."

"Pleasures," said the toenail clippings, "about which we are reluctant to answer questions."

"Pleasures derived from feelings of guilt," said the dust-ruffle.

"Feelings of guilt," said the red carpet, "that allow the pleasure to continue."

"Guilt allows us to continue doing the thing that makes us guilty," said the toenail clippings.

"I feel awful doing this to you," said the dust-ruffle. "I absolutely loathe myself, and yet . . ."

"These bagels are delicious," said Mercy. "The ones with the raisins in them."

"I'm picking out the raisins," said Hallamore. "But for Willy, it must be like a bed of rocks."

"Rocks in my bed," said the red carpet. "A song by Joe Turner."

"Turned into a hash of a song!" said the dust-ruffle.

"Returned to Joe Turner in hash-form," said the Christmas cactus.

"The knees shudder and return," said the red carpet.

"The bones shudder!" said the toenail clippings.

"What is this?" said the Christmas cactus. "This is the woman being liberated from violent male aggression."

"Are you kidding?" said the red carpet. "This is the male hegemony trying to co-opt human experience."

"Yeah," said the dust-ruffle, "here he comes, Mr. Male Hegemony, trying to co-opt human experience."

"Oh Flavio," said the red carpet, "which part of NO didn't you understand?"

"Which part of Kant's *Critique of Judgment* didn't you understand?" said the dust-ruffle.

"Which part of the body didn't you understand?" said the

Even if it doesn't sin, they punish it anyway.

T.V. set.

"Which part of 'whine, whine, complain, complain' didn't you understand?" said the toenail clippings.

"Which part of 'nevertheless, should it, yet, quite moreover, however, perhaps' didn't you understand?" said the Christmas cactus.

"My lip is falling apart at the seams," I said. "That is how chapped it is. I can't open my mouth to answer your questions; I can't open my mouth enough to bite off a mouthful; I can't open enough to kiss you or close enough to kiss you. Putting my mouth on your chin is like eating a pile of salt."

"Speaking, eating, kissing," said Hallamore. "The activities of the mouth. And reading."

"Flavio is the consummate showman," said the T.V. set. "Would you like to see the show, would you like to see the show? Would you like to see what's in Hallamore's magic bag, would you like to see that? Okay, how would you like to see the inside of my mouth? Okay, would you like to see me write a novel in this girl's blood, would you like to see that?"

"It would have to be a short novel," said the dust-ruffle.

"A novella," said the red carpet.

"This isn't literature," said the T.V. set. "This is surgery."

"This isn't civil engineering," said the dust-ruffle. "This is brute violence."

"If you ask me," said the Christmas cactus, "some of the greatest literature comes out of the stove."

"Sometimes we truly fear description," said Mercy. "More often, though, we only pretend to fear description."

"I'm afraid to describe what I have just seen," said Hallamore. "But it makes me feel a lot better about my relationship with my sister."

"It's real," said Mercy. "It's real, it's real, it's real. We have turned our bodies into art. It has become a hideous bloodbath: objects have replaced people. Everyone in this room believes one of these things."

53. Longing for bed

"Imprisoned in sleep, what is Natasha thinking?" said the T.V. set. "Her hand covers her face, obscuring the play of affect. She must be aware of the sheets that surround her and the blankets that seem to hold her in place, preventing her, apparently, from sliding around in bed or sliding out. One of her legs—it would be impossible for her to say which one because she could not be conscious of it without becoming fully conscious—is in a bad position, it is bent at a difficult angle or something, and something is the matter with her toes as well. A murmur of discomfort starting in the area of the toes is collecting somewhere on the inside of the calf, just below the knee. The message is not going to be carried past this point. It will have to remain there; it isn't going to be carried higher in the body where decisions are made. The problem is that on the sleeping body no particular place is very much higher than any other, whereas messages are designed to move up, so that when the body is erect and the legs are straightened out messages have a way of shooting straight to the top, but when the body is supine the messages have no way of getting up there and instead tend to wander back and forth in the corridors where they originate. Natasha must be aware of the problem and probably feels sorry for it and knows that she could repair it by pointing her foot and tensing her leg slightly . . . which would require waking up, so she doesn't bother. She sees it happening but doesn't feel it happen. She feels only the heavy blankets pressing down on her legs and locking them in place. She sees a shape like a black jellybean bobbing against her kneecap, trying to pass through the curve of the knee so that it can get to the place where decisions are made. At last she feels her calf detaching itself from her body, severing its connection to the knee, and sinking into the mattress, as though it were melting and being absorbed by the mattress. Everything falls away. . . . Her highest ambition is to remain unconscious; or she has no ambitions or desires, no charley-horse, no hangnails, no bad taste

163

in her mouth, there is nothing in her stomach. . . . They all say goodbye and immediately dissolve into the mattress. . . ."

54. Red lightning

"I awaken in Natasha's house," I said. "'Good heavens! I'm not supposed to be here,' etc. Can almost hear her moving around upstairs . . . but instead of going out I go upstairs."

"Footsteps on the stairs," said Natasha. "My eyelids flutter, and the background against which I think, the color of the background, changes. With each sound it grows brighter."

"Dark shapes on the landing I thought were slippers," I said. "I tried to put my feet in them and they resisted."

"Willy, your slippers are pathetic," said Natasha. "With each step they paint another sound on the back of my head."

I opened the door.

"Chessboard placed against the window," I said. "Column of heat ascending from the radiator. Shoes pointing away from the bed."

"How does a shoe 'point'?" said Natasha.

"Toes of the shoes pointing away," I said. "Radiator drapes its arm over your chest, clamps its warm hand to your shoulder. As the gas fire on the stove extends its fingers and grasps the saucepan."

"Red lightning behind my eyelids," said Natasha. "Chessboard falls away from the window, turns over, collapses against the radiator and slides off its ribbed back, hits the floor, and rests there."

"A sound: and your understanding of the room has suddenly changed," I said. "The whole room changes. You believe there is someone else in the room."

"I awaken," said Natasha. "My body has changed, and I find an image of myself pressed against me in the bed, arm across my chest, pinning me; I want to push him out, go on, get away, find your own bed, Willy; but I'm too scared to move."

"Not reassuring," I said. "The recurrence of the sound in the room. Hearing it a second time tells you that you certainly heard it the first time, but doesn't change what you learned about the room or about yourself; confirms that you did hear something . . . or that you're really losing your mind, that you hallucinated two sounds instead of one. What if you heard it before it happened?"

"Clang, the radiator raises its voice in alarm," said Natasha. "I open my eyes. Lightning suspends the room in a red medium. Centipede hurrying down the wall stops where the shine on its back reflects my worried image."

"Are you reassured by what you see?" I said. "What did you want to see? Did you want to see a centipede there?"

"Red lightning," said Natasha. "A sound I saw as a color. (The radiator again.)"

55. You looked frightened.
   What were you running from?

"Why should you be afraid of me?" said Natasha. "You know very well I don't exist."

"I should be afraid of you," I said. "But I'm not."

"You want me to frighten you. You're looking for . . . reasons to be afraid of me. You want me to provide one for you."

"Do I need a reason to be afraid of you?"

"Are you saying your fear is irrational?"

"Did I say I was afraid?"

"I'm pleased that you feel threatened by my elegant conversation."

"What's behind this wall?"

"Fear of white brick? What if the brick wall says: 'Why are you afraid of me when you know I don't exist?'"

"You frighten me, but I can't take you seriously."

"Come here."

"The bed. The quilt. The 'comforter.' I have a problem with beds."

"That's when you feel the tiredness hit you and the bed starts to look especially good."

"A wave of tiredness just hit me in the chest."

"I can tell. You look kind of . . . out of focus."

"I don't know if I'm in bed or not."

"Thank you so much for giving me an insight into your mind."

"How do I know that you don't exist? What makes you think I know this?"

"What are you afraid of? What if the cup of tea says: 'I don't exist'? What if the beer bottle says it? The ashtray? What if the T.V. set wants to know: 'Why are you afraid of me?' The telephone? (Why are you afraid of the telephone?)"

"This bed is infested."

"No, it's only the special admiration fleas have for you."

"A good enough reason to be afraid of you, that smile. Another reason: the sound of your voice."

"Kiss."

"If you kiss me like that, then we can't talk any more."

"Come back, sleep! The bed misses you."

"Do you mean me?"

"I'm trying to entice my sleep back into bed."

"I'm incapable of sleeping with your biology teacher in the bed."

"I can't sleep without him. I've grown accustomed to seeing a certain number of slides of the inner ear before falling asleep."

56. Image projected onto a bed

"It doesn't take very many slides of the inner ear to put me to sleep," said Hallamore.

"I never want to sleep here again," said Natasha. "Well, how dare they violate our incest?"

"You've been bedridden too long," said Mercy. "The bed rides by night; by day it rests."

"I feel as though I've been ridden by night," said Natasha.

"I've written a novel by night," I said. "*To Be Read by Night, a novel.* I did it on slices of bread that glow with a rose-colored light for you to read it by."

"In my dream, a small gray dog kept biting his tail," said Natasha. "He was pulling hairs out. I held him and tried to calm him, but when I let go of his head he started snapping at his tail again."

"You were pulling hairs out of the dog's tail?" I said.

"What must you think of me? He was pulling them out of his own tail," said Natasha. "I think you were the dog, Willy. He was wearing your glasses."

"He wants to be petted," said Mercy, "he wants to be fed, he gets jealous easily, he's worried when you leave, and he couldn't open a door to save his life."

"He wants to get into bed but something tells him he shouldn't," said Hallamore. "And fleas find him interesting."

I was unthreatening . . . but harmless? And I thought for the first time in years of my friend the surgeon. I had never felt completely sure of her, but I knew that she took me seriously because she made fun of me, because she knew me well enough to make fun of me, whereas my biology teacher always addressed me formally because he didn't take me seriously. She used to offer, whenever she saw me, to perform an operation on my eyes to eliminate my reading block, and eventually her persistence won me over to the extent that I allowed her to remove from my eye something that she called an impurity. But I had never made an appointment for the follow-up operation on the other eye; I was not convinced that her efforts so far had actually corrected my vision, which sometimes seemed less trustworthy than before. I was even starting to suspect that the piece she had removed from my eye was something I really needed. So much of trusting another person was the idea that she trusted you, but where did this idea come from? If I trusted my eyesight, if I knew that what I saw was no different from what anyone else saw, how, exactly, did I know this? Maybe there was a kind of exchange that took place between cities, so that information about an event could sometimes reach a city before the event took place in another city. Maybe, if my surgeon cut me open, reached inside, removed part of me that was rotten, and stitched me up, we would know it in St. Paul before it happened in Minneapolis. Or what if it never happened? What if it took place between cities? On the phone?

57. Private way dangerous passing
(for John Pitcher)

She had asked more than once: When was I coming to see her. And I had taken that to mean: that she was expecting me, imagining what it would be like to have me there. She had, I thought, already cleared a space for me, at least in her mind if not in her house. I thought that because I thought about it all the time, it had already happened. Or perhaps I felt that my feeling had been communicated because I felt it so strongly. I thought that what I wanted would come to me because I wanted it very much. I seemed to think that my expectations would be realized if I entertained them without acting on them. Certainly I had thought that because my feelings were so strong, they would be reciprocated. I had thought—but how can a thought communicate itself?—that she would be waiting for me. At last I knew that she was not waiting, and my knowledge took the form of tears.

I got off the bus and started to cry. I didn't know what to do with myself: The last of my money was spent; the people I knew well were out of town, perhaps for the winter; I was in a part of the city that I did not recognize and could not place in relation to anything I knew (for instance, where was the river?). The doctor I had come so far to see, a woman who worked at the veterans's hospital as a surgeon, failed to meet me at the terminal, and not only because she was absentminded. In the flurry of excitement in which I left—because I had been thinking about leaving for a long time, and then left on something like a whim—I had neglected to inform her of my visit.

At that time the idea of giving up something that was important to me was so important to me that I couldn't give it up. Recently I had given up drinking tea. There was no reason for drinking tea in America, my sister maintained, tea was an affectation. That was when I was in the habit of drinking as many as nine cups a day; so I gave it up. I also gave up my job in the theater company where I had worked for five years; stopped practicing piano, which I had taken up in the first place only to please my wife; sold off most of my books, which turned out not to be worth all that much; separated from my wife and left most of my things with her (not such a generous act, this legacy: What was she going to do with it?); and stopped calling my sister. I was paring down, purifying myself, keeping close to me only those things that I thought my friend would appreciate. If she had said that she thought a certain color was good for me, I held on to things of that color. If she had said to me, she liked me in that shirt, I held on to that shirt; I was wearing it now. I stepped down from the bus, wearing the shirt she liked, saw that she was not there, accepted my suitcase from the man who was offering it to me and saying the same thing he was saying to everyone else—and I gave her up. Now what?

Now I was standing in front of a house that I thought was hers. The lights were out and the windows were curtained and shaded. Almost out of habit, I called to mind the thought of her hands, her surgeon's hands that could enter your body at any point. And I closed and opened my eyes to see if the world had changed in the interim. It was a fine night. My unwieldy suitcase was buried in the snow a few feet away, full of things that were of no use to me: I was glad to be rid of it, even for a moment. I had come a long way from the bus station but still didn't know quite where I was, although I was in a city that I knew my way around in, having been born there and gone to school there. But I had just come from another city, and my mind was still trying to navigate the streets of that city in a way that would allow me not to run into anyone I was trying to avoid. For some reason I was always running away from people in that other city; there seemed to be a lot of people there who wanted something from me or thought that I owed them something that I had no desire to give them. Now I was in my native city and I was still running from them, taking the long way because it seemed safer, keeping off the streets where in the past I had run into the wrong person, looking ahead without seeing anything because I didn't want to see the faces I was expecting.

Result: I couldn't be sure that it was her house. Clearly she was not home—clearly no one was, so I turned to the right and somehow ended up in one of the houses in that direction.

The house I ended up in belonged to the sculptor Leslie Oram, a friend of my surgeon friend's. She let me in, although she didn't really like me, with a smile that was a little like a handlebar mustache. She had a way of expressing concern about me that showed that she didn't like me too much—she professed to be worried about me, but the worry wasn't causing her any pain. She was worried about me, she would say, she hadn't seen me in a long time, and she would smile when she said that; she was really delighted to see how badly things were going for me, and even more delighted not to have seen me for so long. The reason why Leslie didn't like me, my friend the surgeon told me, was that she did not like men, although I knew that this was kind of an overstatement, since there were some men she liked to do things with, and I was, I thought, no less likeable than they. There were boyfriends, too, whom she had gone out with for a while, but it's possible that she never liked them.

Her dislike gave me a certain advantage, which I was determined not to use. Her dislike of me always took the form of concern; therefore asking her to let me in would be the same as saying: Tell me to come in. The question seemed to offer her a choice, but when she tried to answer it she would realize that she had no choice, because actually I had eliminated all the choices except for the one I wanted. Or I could give her a long list of choices (could I stay at her place for the night, or did she know anywhere else I could stay, or did she think it was totally inappropriate to ask, or was there not any room in the house, or was I disturbing her work), I could even give her a list of excuses for not letting me in, and it would come out the same; it was the same as pretending to give her a choice while tacitly indicating the one she was supposed to pick, and I was determined not to confer an obligation by presenting it as a choice. But maybe it's inevitable; maybe anyone confers an obligation on you by knocking on the door in the middle of the night, especially if it's a man you don't like with a dislike that disguises itself as tender care. It isn't easy to throw him out of the house; it isn't easy to get anyone out of your house, even if you want it very much; you dream of a time when you will be alone in your own house, you look forward with an attitude of almost pornographic anticipation to a time when you will be alone, deliciously vulnerable, and afraid. How safe you feel when a man you don't like is sleeping in your house, or a house you may be borrowing from a friend. He makes everything nauseatingly safe, patrolling the halls while you sleep, closing all the cabinets one by one (a door won't close: He presses on it until he is satisfied that something on the other side is sticking out, pressing back; he leaves it open), and he fixes things, untangles the phone cord, and washes everything in the sink. Then he leaves while you're still sleeping, and manages to lock the door behind him without using a key, and the only evidence that he was there is the cheery note magnetized to the side of the refrigerator: Leslie! Thanks so much/ Sculpture of cat four stars/ ★ ★ ★ ★ (highest rating)/ Best wishes/ William. You were thinking that you might have dreamed he was there, but strangely you don't feel any better about him.

I slept badly that night until someone kicked me in the stomach. It turned out to be Leslie's new boyfriend Jim Vanek, who had gotten a little turned around on the way out and seemed to be slightly drunk. I was unable to explain how I had come to be in a place where he could trip over me. He seemed prepared to assume that I was the second boyfriend and that I had entered the house to seduce Leslie with the gift of a kitten; his other idea was that I was the old boyfriend and had broken in in the middle of the night, using my own key, which I was not supposed to have, intending to take my cat back (something must have given him the idea that a cat was involved, probably the relief sculpture of a curled-up cat done in a piece of marble on the floor not far from where I had made my bed). I found these scenarios hard to resist because his ideas about what I might be doing in this house were so much clearer than mine—and, besides, they were a little flattering, because I had always believed that Leslie didn't like me, whereas according to Jim's way of thinking it was possible that she did. Not at all, I insisted, everyone agreed: She hated my guts. People were telling me this all the time, when her name came up, she hated my

"Your voice brings me back to life, which wasn't necessarily something I wanted."

guts—shaking their heads, smiling as though they were doing me a favor, as though I could use this information. And I did not want to depend on anyone for anything, I went on (hoping, perhaps, that I would not win this argument), it wasn't good to depend too much on a person, a drink, a machine, a profession, a pastime; or if I did have to depend on someone, I wanted to choose the person—in fact, I had chosen someone and told her I depended on her for so many things and had ceased to depend on anyone else, but she had left me (I actually said "left me" although she must have left before I got there). I felt like Hektor deserted by Apollo, I told him, suddenly made aware of things he needed, had not thought to relinquish, and could not imagine losing, when, in a terrible moment, he was deprived of them. There was nothing else I could imagine losing, not because I had lost everything but because I had reached a point at which my imagination failed. I had always lived in houses: Could houses abandon me? I had always had enough to eat: Could food abandon me? I had always depended on others to protect me, and I had given up on them one by one, and now I had to depend on Leslie, but at least I could depend on her to this extent: She did not begrudge me something to eat and a small corner to sleep in, even if she hated my guts.

When given a choice, I have always preferred the unknown to the known. I was basically familiar with the difficulties that attended my stay in Leslie's house; I could predict them, I knew all about them, whereas Jim represented to me a set of unforeseeable difficulties, and, after all, there were difficulties everywhere, so I left her a note and followed him home. I was welcome to stay, he said he was going to California for two weeks and needed someone to watch the house, take care of the cat, water the plants if it looked like they needed it; he wasn't offering money, of course, but it would be a favor to him and it might also solve my problem. Otherwise he was going to put the cat in a carrying case and take him on the plane and give him a pill to knock him out, and he didn't like to do it. He told me this while holding the door to let me in the house—not an ordinary house but a divided house, a duplex; he was renting. He was moving—if I wanted to take over the lease—to

California, actually; his wife, a film editor, really needed to be there for her work. His wife? Mercy Carbonell, unspeakable coincidence; she was doing something in the kitchen when we came in. William Fucking Kunin, she exclaimed when she recognized me, as though fucking were a middle name or as though the whole thing were a terrible curse; she might have been surprised and pleased or surprised and outraged, and both possibilities, from my point of view, were disturbing. I hadn't seen her since, probably, the time she was panhandling outside a bookstore and said (addressing me) buddy, could she have five dollars for a copy of *Cyrano* so that she could continue her interrupted education. Anyone else, anyone who knew her, would have bought her lunch at least, but I hadn't— something that I wasn't proud of, but I wasn't beating myself up about it—because she said *Cyrano*, because that was her concept of education. She could have said Emmanuel Levinas, she could have said Michael Cunningham, who I think is deplorable, worse than Edmond Rostand who is safely dead, and I would have bought her the book and taken her out to lunch, but Rostand was the kind of thing that appealed to her, so naturally when she thought about educating herself the textbook she envisioned was Rostand. Seeing her again brought back my failure of sympathy, which remained an indictment of my character because I still couldn't sympathize with her; but that hadn't prevented her from becoming totally bourgeois, a film editor even, with a mathematician for a husband, and a small son named, apparently in remembrance of me, Will. I wondered if she still had the letters I had written her, the poems . . . one poem in particular of which I had tried to collect and destroy every remaining copy, but one was still unaccounted for. It pained me to think that a copy of that poem, a copy from which others could be made, was still floating around somewhere with my name on it. Maybe she had destroyed it. I had destroyed everything of hers that it was in my power to destroy—letters, books, other gifts, except for some candy which I had passed along to my sister and which she had consumed—but then again, that was the kind of thing that appealed to me. The idea of destroying something that I no longer loved, burning it so that pieces of it went into the air (air

177

that she breathed: a way of returning her letters to her), appealed to me on a very deep level.

There was no reason for me to be there, my wife asserted. I had called her mainly to confirm my belief that she was not good for me. It was the first thing I said when I came in, nodding to Mercy without saying hello: I needed to use the phone, I would use my calling card. It was my sister's calling card, which she had given me in case I needed to call her, and I had gotten very good at saying, in a way the machine could recognize, calling card, and typing the number, but I had really been using it to call my wife in the hope that her unkind words would establish that I was better off without her. Giving her up had been relatively easy after I had given up my job as a member of the corps of the theater in which she was a part-owner. I had been working as a dancer for several years and was now too old to continue but had never been suited to this kind of work. I should have been a professor of some kind, an English teacher, a historian, a philosopher. One of my teachers used to complain that my movements tended to have a certain academic quality, because they all had the same awkward look of my deliberation, because it took such a long time for me to learn a dance, because nothing came naturally to me as a dancer and I had to be conscious of every part of what I was doing all the time. Oh, so I was a professor, was I, Jim interrupted. What of. He had apparently not been listening closely and I was almost grateful. I told him I was working (if he thought it was work; it was work, he assured me) on a monograph on Thomas Traherne. It was true that I had Traherne's *Centuries of Meditations* in my suitcase and had read some of it; it looked interesting. However, at that time the act of reading was still extremely painful to me because of the opening in my eye which my friend the surgeon had created and forgotten to close. Because the eye that had been operated on had never healed satisfactorily, it could not absorb words very easily; it could only release them. One eye was always releasing words while the other was trying to absorb them, so that I could not distinguish, when I had a book in front of me, between the words that were on the page, offering themselves up for inspection, and the words that were pouring out of my eye and crowding the others out. And this was also what I understood Traherne to be saying, except that I could not tell whether the idea was being expressed by Traherne or whether it was flowing out of my eye. I understood Traherne to be saying that everything in this book, given to me by my surgeon friend, was going to come out of my eye; the contents of my head were going to pass through my eye and drain into the book. When my head was empty I would be happy. I was happy once; then my teachers put centipedes in my head, and the centipedes devoured the happiness. I had learned to worry: what was my education if not the gradual replacement of happiness by worry? What was I looking for in this book if not a surface on which to spread my worry or a receptacle to contain it?

In the kitchen, all the cabinets were open: boxes of some cracker in one of them, books in another, an instruction manual for operating an IBM work-station, another instruction manual. It unnerved me; I wanted to close them. And no one had taken out the garbage or changed the sand in the catbox for some time because neither of them was going to be the first one to do it. When I crossed the room, Mercy followed me, stepping around the dishwasher, which was also open. So she and I had gone to the same school, Jim was saying, did we have a lot of classes together. No, we had just had, she said, a lot of sex together. And I had written her some letters and poems which later she used to read over and over again when she was living on the street (not quite on the street: in a minibus, which could hardly be made to go but which locked securely). When we were in school I had written closely-written letters; we had fooled around briefly, in secret; she had repented, thought of her boyfriend; I had written new letters, double-spaced, filling every available space on the page, filling the margins with dingbats and squirly-gigs so that there was no space on the page that did not express my intention, using every letter-writing trick I could think of; the boyfriend had been sacked; and I had been promoted to his place. She was the only person I had ever pursued, except for the ones I had pursued in a halting, desultory, self-questioning manner; but this one time I had been active, sure of myself, had made myself interesting, had mobilized my resources, deployed them, and it had worked wonderfully well. And then one day I stopped pursuing her, withdrew my attentions; for me it was as though a veil had been removed exposing everything that was wrong with her that others, primarily my sister, had objected to. That was the end of my letter-writing career. Then Mercy went away somewhere, returned, lived on the street, sometimes dropping by the house where I was living with my sister, meanwhile sending letters nearly every day for about a year, which I saved in a grapefruit box and then destroyed.

I didn't think there was anything unusual about my behavior toward Mercy. I believed that I was normal, that other people were like me. My assumption, despite all evidence to the contrary, was always that what I saw and felt was universal; I refused to believe that things affected me in a unique way. I believed that others were lying when they said they weren't like me, when they claimed they enjoyed things that I didn't enjoy, when they imagined what I couldn't see. And I didn't exactly believe that she had become a film editor. I didn't know anything about it, but I thought that it involved marking film with a kind of pencil, cutting the film to pieces with a kind of scissors, re-attaching the pieces with something, and running it through a machine—what they called a moviola?—to do something to it; and I knew that she was not good with her hands, or with machines either; so I assumed, when they referred to her work as a film editor, that they were speaking figuratively. Probably she imagined herself as a film editor (which is not the same as wanting to be one: I had always imagined myself as a professor at a college; I really thought that I might have been up to it).

Early the next morning, Mercy was entering the spare bedroom where I had cleared a small space for myself and made a pallet on the floor. Now I could hear her selecting some heavy object from a shelf and setting it down, scraping the floor a little, sliding it into the hall, easing the door shut, making her way downstairs—all of these actions and their attendant sounds seemed to be directed at me, but I didn't know how to interpret them—slamming the kitchen door, trying several keys in the lock before getting the one

that worked, then slamming the trunk of the car and asking if Jim
had remembered to bring the coffee; I did not hear his reply. I
remained in my homemade bed for a long time after that, trying to
sleep although I wasn't tired, because I didn't want to see them if
they came back for something or if by some chance they were still
in the house. When at last I got up and looked around the spare
bedroom, they seemed to be gone. It wasn't much of a bedroom; it
was more like a garage . . . walls lined with shelves, cardboard boxes
on the floor, things she was saving, packets of important papers
(her work seemed to require a lot of documentation). She kept
other things in the spare bedroom too, stuff that I recognized from
our time together, little gifts that I had made, and other artifacts
which I don't know how she ended up with. Probably all of my old
drawings and paintings, most of them inspired by illustrations I
had seen in the newspaper, were on the shelves in the room where I
was supposed to be sleeping, except that I found it difficult to sleep
in the shadow of those shelves and boxes. The fact is that I wasn't
actually doing any of the things that I was supposed to be doing at
the time. I was supposed to be looking for work and a place of my
own, and I wasn't doing that. I was supposed to be sleeping in the
spare bedroom with the results, such as they were, of my artistic
endeavors—and how could I possibly do that?

One week later Mercy showed up at the door and I had to
let her in because I had locked the door from the inside. Stupid
of me not to have noticed where it was written on the calendar by
the refrigerator, in the square marked out for today, that Mercy was
supposed to return. Again I called my wife but was interrupted by
a call on the other line which turned out to be Jim in California;
he refused to believe that I was still living in his house, and insisted
that it was Mercy imitating my voice and manner. When finally I
got back to the conversation with my wife I was reassured to hear
her put it to me that there was still no reason for me to be there,
which gave me one reason, at least, to stay where I was. Instead
I went outside for the first time in several days—I had gone out
more than once early in my stay and had even found an apartment
only to have Leslie tell me, with a malicious smile, when I ran into

her on the way to sign the lease, that it was in a building that was bookended by crack houses. I was not sure whether to believe her or not, but I didn't have money to pay the rent anyway, so I broke the lease and went back to Mercy's house and went through her things and removed and destroyed anything that looked familiar, anything that had my name on it, anything that reminded me of me; I also got rid of some of the clutter and had pushed most of the appliances and boxes of stuff into the main bedroom and closed the door when suddenly Mercy appeared and forced me outside again.

I had not been walking for more than an hour when I ran into my great friend Bernard Hallamore. This was extraordinary luck because he was really the only person who could have helped me then, the only one whose help I would have accepted; I did not realize that I was looking for him until I saw him waiting outside the music library. Because he knew me through others, he didn't know, at first, how to talk to me in their absence: Where was Natasha, he asked, where was Nora, and I felt for a second like a severed limb. His enthusiasm on finding out that Nora and I had split up; my own elation at his apparent enthusiasm (not having to apologize for something that, I knew, I had handled very badly); his even greater delight on finding that I was thinking about having more corrective surgery for my reading block, which he recommended heartily. Then he emptied out his briefcase and showed me, in quick succession, a photograph of his grandmother, several notecards (the results of his attempts to fit everything he knew on a notecard), and a letter from an eleven-year-old girl living in London whom he described as his fiancée: She would not marry him, she wrote in the letter, unless he shaved his beard. He had shaved, I noticed, the absurd beard that used to run along the edge of his jaw in a narrow line like the strap of a helmet. Then, without any prompting, he invited me to stay with him and became almost violent when he discovered that I was staying with his sister: Merciful heavens! That was no place to stay. Hallamore had lived with her once—he said "lived with," but that did not express his position in her household very well, since it was, after all, "her household" that he had been connected to. The connection between him and her household was delicate; he often had the feeling that she was on the verge of telling him to get out, and this feeling probably led to some awkwardness. Well, it was awkward for both of them. They eventually developed a system—every house was basically a system—it was hard to say what their system was, because they had arranged everything so that they never knew what they had arranged; one of the terms of their extraordinarily awkward arrangement seemed to be that they must never articulate the terms, as though the act of saying what the terms were would cause the house to vanish. Then Hallamore took me to his apartment on Dupont and fed me a goulash that wasn't bad and got out his T.V. so that we could watch David Letterman but the reception was not good, and we stayed up most of the night talking.

The first thing I saw the next morning was a small square of newsprint pasted at eye-level, if you were lying down, on the wall by the bed: a reproduction of an Arnold Schoenberg self-portrait painted around the time when he was giving up tonality. But he never gave up the human figure in painting, although here he had painted his own head a light blue: more of a modernist, then, as a composer, if a modernist is someone who makes art out of renunciation. The words "will you renounce," a quotation from something, or a sentence from my dream, were in my head as I rose from Hallamore's narrow bed, bathed in his ancient bathtub (the apartment was quite old; no shower had ever been put in), put on one of the shirts that he always looked so comfortable in, breakfasted on muffins that he had made and yogurt that disappointed him because it was not brown—its natural color, he said. In my dream I had taken up smoking, something I had been careful never to do in life and had never even tried because it frightened me, because I thought that I was prone to it. Had I reached a point at which I was going to have to take something up in order to continue renouncing things?

I spent the rest of the day following Hallamore as he made his rounds. He lived "like a monk" (his own words), but a monk who had dedicated himself to every kind of pleasure. Each day had a precise schedule of lunches, coffees, walks, and sittings; he made appearances (like a nineteenth-century person of fashion "showing" himself) at Dunn Brothers's, Savran's, the post office, the Rainbow Chinese restaurant, various libraries. There was, in each of these places, a different woman he was either flirting with or sleeping with. For example: His appearance at the music library, where he practiced harpsichord, was timed to coincide with Arethusa's. (How, I wondered, could he be so callous about Arethusa? She looked at me admiringly, then unbelievingly, when I told her simply that I knew him.) He was going to finish his degree in music for real this time, he said: He was going to get the degree, sleep with more women, improve his golf game, and not lose any more hair. He had dropped out of school once before to take a job as an organist in a church, but he had lost the job as a result of sleeping through too many services, and then had done almost nothing for several years.

We saw a movie that night with Fred Jodry, who was the director of the choir in the church where Hallamore used to play the organ and whose sexuality was equally predatory. We agreed that the movie was bad but the house in the movie was perfect; there was no way the characters could be so miserable when they lived in that house. The house was perfect because it did not make false statements about itself or the extent of its rooms. The walls in the house were bare, so that if you ran into a wall you knew there was nothing behind it; it didn't pretend to be another room or an outside. Fred maintained that the purpose of decoration was to conceal cruelty, and Hallamore observed that nothing in that house would allow you to forget about the cruelty and suffering that are the fabric of life, and I agreed that suffering was the only valid kind of aesthetic experience. We then revised our opinion: The house was perfect because it highlighted the misery of the characters; we agreed that we should all be made to suffer. Then we compared recordings of "Five Piano Pieces" by Schoenberg, and Fred and Hallamore agreed that the Glenn Gould interpretation was superior to the one by Maurizio Pollini, and I also agreed with them. Then I explained my plan to become a better reader and showed them the book by Traherne that my friend the surgeon had given me. I told them what she had said and how I had taken it to mean that she was waiting for me, that she would put me up until I found another place to stay. I supposed that she had waited during the time when I was planning to visit her for the operation on my second eye. I knew that she had been having a bad time of it then, because of her job and the people she was living with, who were unsympathetic, and because she was hiding so many things from a number of people—including me, as I gathered later. I sometimes thought about calling or writing to say that I was coming, but never called or sent any letter because it seemed as though that would be pushing it a little. I even invented some reasons for calling: I had lost her address or needed directions, an obvious lie. . . . If I had called, Fred remarked, it would have been unnecessary for her to give me the information, since she would have offered to pick me up when I arrived. Right, I said, but I didn't want her to see that I was capable of lying about something inconsequential, didn't want her to think that what I was lying about was more significant than it really was—better, in that case, not to call, not to make a nuisance of myself. And I didn't write letters anymore; I had given that up years ago.

At breakfast the next morning Hallamore told me sadly that I couldn't stay at his place that night and probably not for a couple of nights after that; his biology teacher and other mentors were coming to town and he had to put them up, but he thought he might be able to get me into Bob Scholes's house. This proposal appealed to me for reasons that I did not care to admit. I often used to see Professor Scholes around town, and he would nod and wave hello to me, mistaking me, I think, for someone else, which never bothered me, although I knew that he and Professor Spilka, who also possessed a round face, bright eyes, white beard, and brown fedora, were often mistaken for each other, and this infuriated them. Spilka I also used to see from time to time, but he never took any notice of me and seemed very wrapped up in his own concerns, perhaps contemplating yet another monograph on D. H. Lawrence. But Scholes meant something to me; his friendly greetings suggested a generous nature. Thus it was "perfect," as Hallamore said with a relieved expression that he did not bother to conceal.

That Professor Scholes would be away from his house did not occur to me until we were there and Hallamore was introducing me to Eleanor Kaufman, who was housesitting for her teacher and also preparing the index for his new book. The house was large, she said, and mostly empty, so there were plenty of rooms to choose from; she put me in the one that she called the blue room, the ceiling of which was blue. But the ceiling was almost entirely blotted out by the dark wood frame and canopy of the bed, surely the most enormous bed I had ever seen, which dominated the room, interrupting the path of the door if you tried to open it all the way. Hallamore left, and I spent several hours pacing the narrow corridor between the bed and the wall because I did not want to go down into the kitchen while Eleanor was using it. My body had a tendency to wander away from the bed on which I had placed Traherne's *Centuries of Meditations;* suddenly I was in the closet and my book was in another room. I circled the bed in circles that expanded and became irregular until they were no longer recognizable as circles. Objects of interest pulled me away; I was possessed by a desire to pick up an object that I kept seeing on the edges of my elliptical orbit. The edges of the room seemed to be alive with a lot of priapic statuary, a bronze centaur rearing up to show off his erection, a ceramic Humpty Dumpty buggering a ceramic pumpkin that had no face, all of these naughty little garden-gods projecting from the walls, from the legs and columns of the bed, into the center of the room; I was disturbed by this. The bed pulled at me to lie down on the bed. Food pulled at me. . . . Meanwhile in another room Eleanor was doing something else, eating or preparing to eat, opening the refrigerator, setting the ingredients on the counter, arranging them in a line, cooking them on the stove, running some machinery, and I could hear her perfectly. I continued in my circuit, following the pattern in the carpet into the closet or the bathroom, marching in time, at first unconsciously and then with mounting irritation, to the rhythm determined by Wagner's *Siegfried,* which was playing somewhere in the house, seemingly above my head, until I had had enough and at midnight went down the back stairs into the kitchen and ate part of Eleanor's dinner—very good, excellent, which was not surprising since she had spent nearly six hours preparing it.

That night I awoke under a terrible weight. I could not roll it off, but at last I was able to crawl out from under it, fall out of bed, turn on the lamp. It was Bob Scholes, the literary critic! Unless it was Mark Spilka, who, lost on the way home from a conference about D. H. Lawrence, confused, had wandered into the wrong house. He looked awful. His pants were unzipped, and he didn't even have a shirt on; his long white beard was greasy and awry in places . . . but when we talked, he was surprisingly lucid. I showed him some of the mistakes I had identified in Wagner's *Siegfried.* It was nothing much, some errors of historical fact, discontinuities, the untenable ideas about metallurgy, etc. He listened sympathetically. I told him that I felt . . . guilty for catching mistakes in Wagner. Catching mistakes in Wagner, he told me, meant that I was spending too much time with it, listening to it too closely.

I went down the stairs and out the door, dragging my unwieldy suitcase behind me, wishing for a surgeon, a surgeon to heal my wounds. I was uncertain . . . but unhappy? More information was required to give my feeling some direction. My surgeon: Was I ever on her list? Would it have been possible? Was I truly mistaken or had I only failed to act? Missed my chance? Was there a moment when everything changed? (Could I recall it?) I was going to be unhappy in any case: did it have to be imprecise? A vague feeling?

My mind would not let go of the image of her hands, which it had endowed with an ability to pass through solids; I imagined her hand passing through my eye without disturbing its composition. The cold and my distance from her only magnified my fantasy; I was in a state of heightened desire, brought on by her absence, which would have been dispelled by the slightest touch; and I also had a desire for sleep without the ability to sleep.

It was still dark out; the street was empty. Newspapers were starting to appear on the doorsteps. Good to be alive, I said, good

Aaron Kunin

to be alive, but I didn't mean it. I would sleep in the bus station . . .
sleep that devours memory, that consumes experience.

No ice was safe, said the sign by the pond. That was certainly
true, I agreed, as I lost my balance and fell, waving my arms wildly,
into the sidewalk.

All this happened in Minneapolis.

Like the horse that carries on its back what it will eat.

INDEX

See also: Carbonell, Mercy; shame-artist, the
Bible, the, 17
bicycle, the, 49, 50, 102
Big Joe Turner
    See: Turner, Joe
biology teacher, the, 5, 22, 25, 34, 35, 37, 44-45, 50-51, 58, 105,
    134, 135, 155, 158, 159, 168, 169, 185; called "Valla," 34;
    fails to save Mercy from mistakes, 51, 135; in restroom,
    50-58; prohibits time spent in bakery, 22; sleeps, 45, 168;
    vacations in Miami, 50
Boehlke, Bain, 35
books, 12, 20, 29, 50, 58, 59, 65, 67, 68, 73, 76, 97, 110, 124, 129,
    130, 137-41, 150, 158, 172, 177, 178-79, 182, 185, 186;
    indistinct/invisible, 137-38; nauseating, 137, 139, 177;
    toxic, 137; unreadable, 67, 137-41, 178-79, 186
bowtie, the, impossible in Minneapolis, 116-17
brain, the, 7, 44, 62, 71, 93, 94, 151
Brazil, 34
bread, 21, 22, 23, 31, 37, 43-44, 64, 74, 104, 169
Brecht, Bertholt, quoted, 87
Brontë, Charlotte, 67, 68
Brubeck, Dave, 7
bus, the, 40, 171, 172, 185, 188

cabinets, 22, 90, 96, 174, 179
cakes, 21, 22, 23, 98; illiterate, 23; made with salt, 23
California, 176-77, 181
camels, 146, 159
Carbonell, Mercy, accepts ride from biology teacher, 50-51;
    conceals love for Hallamore, 7, 44-45; delicate beauty of,
    58; disturbed by food preparation, 22, 92; eats an apple,
    5, 58; falls through window, 131-36; homeless, 177, 179;
    ideas about art, 12, 94, 105-106, 116-17; impersonates
    Natasha, 122; infatuation with newspaper, 76-77;
    infatuation with Willy, 48, 57, 71, 120-26, 177-80; lives in
    abandoned vending machine warehouse, 91; mistaken

consciousness, 6, 28, 29, 33, 34, 35, 37, 51, 53, 81, 89, 91, 92, 93-
94, 125, 177, 163, 169, 175, 178, 187
cookies, 22, 30, 71, 147
crack, 101, 182
Critique of Judgment (Kant), 117, 160
crumbs, 57, 104, 138
Cunningham, Michael, representative of deplorable tendencies in
the novel, 177
Curry House
See: Sri Lanka Curry House, the
Cyrano (Rostand), 177

dance, 28, 178
dead, the, 8, 28, 34, 43, 45, 64, 104, 176
death, 8, 11, 18, 19, 20, 27-28, 31-32, 42, 63, 64, 90, 138, 139;
literary d., 139
decisions, 23, 98-99, 107, 110, 111, 138; failure to make d.
becomes d., 99; on the way to a d., 107
defenestration, of Mercy, 131-36; of novel, 139-40; of Willy, 139
See also: Carbonell, Mercy; Kunin, William; novel, the;
windows
de Havilland, Olivia, 76
Descartes, René, poets attempted assassination of, 19
description, inadequate, 135; incapacity for, 64, 106-108; fear
of, 162; of bakery, 21-22; of bedroom, 130, 147, 165,
183, 186; of book, 137-40; of centipede, 82, 146; of
door, 50; of Hallamore, 43, 44-45, 135, 182; of house, 186-
87; of kitchen, 91; of living room, 100, 105; of Mercy,
46, 48, 131, 132-35; of Minneapolis, 46-47, 130, 172; of
Natasha, 56, 156-57, 159, 163-64; of newspaper, 70, 71,
73-74, 81-82; of restaurant, 50; of shame-artist, 108-11;
of Scholes/Spilka, 185-86, 187; of sky, 130; of umbrella,
42-43; of Willy, 46-47, 124, 135, 136, 152, 169
dialectic, 13, 45
dogs, 7, 13, 35, 52, 60, 169
Don Giovanni, 35-36

184; rejected by Erin McGonagle, 114, 116; rejected by
Leah Gelpe, 22, 23, 44; rejected by Mercy, 5, 7, 9, 44-45,
146; rejected by household objects, 148, 152; rejected
by nature, 16-17; rejects Willy, 40-41; sleeps on Mercy's
sofa, 42, 43, 98, 100-101; throws Coke can at Saul Bellow,
111-13; trucking company, 20; untroubled by fleas, 52-54
hardness, 5, 8, 9, 13, 16, 32, 38, 96, 130, 137, 151, 159, 162, 163
hats, 5, 13, 43, 61, 76, 84, 93-94, 145-46, 182; made of newspaper,
76; lined with newspaper, 93; paper bag worn as h., 146;
resemblance to umbrella, 43; stolen from trustee, 146
head, the, 5, 6, 11, 12, 13, 17, 22, 24, 29, 33, 38, 43, 59, 68, 71,
81, 85, 91, 93-94, 105, 107, 108, 112, 113, 125, 130, 131,
132, 134, 137, 144, 146, 165, 169, 176, 179, 183, 187;
called "doghouse," 93; compared to doughnut, 93;
emptiness of, 93-94, 112, 137, 179; seen from behind, 5,
93-94; blows to the h., 6, 91, 112-13, 134, 137
See also: artist of the h., the
The Heiress (Wyler), 76
Hektor, 176
Hill, James J., 41
Hippolyte et Aricie (Rameau), 116-17
Hospital Corners (vending machine), 98-100; sings, 100
"Hound of the Baskervilles" (Doyle), 35
house, the, 5, 9, 10, 16-18, 27, 34, 39, 46, 50, 51, 52, 56, 63, 73,
76, 78-79, 81, 83, 91, 93, 101, 107, 108, 120, 130, 131, 132,
135, 136, 148, 165, 171, 172, 173, 174, 176, 180, 181-82,
183, 184, 185, 186, 187; complains, 16-18; crack h., 182; h.
as system, 136, 183; method of dealing with vermin, 16
housesitting, 51, 176-77, 186

idea, 6, 20, 23, 24, 27, 28, 29, 32-33, 37, 41, 46, 64, 72, 80, 82, 91-
92, 93, 104, 108, 126, 158, 168, 171, 174, 177, 179, 187;
dissolved in tea, 104; distinguished from thought, 29;
forgiveness for i., 108; tendency to degenerate, 93, 126
images, 3, 5, 6, 7, 8, 9, 11, 13, 15, 16, 17, 21, 22, 23, 24, 25, 26, 28,
29, 30, 34, 37, 38, 39, 40, 41, 45, 46-48, 49, 50, 52, 54, 55,

59, 61, 65, 66, 67, 69, 71, 72, 73, 74, 78, 80, 82, 84, 87, 90,
91, 92, 93, 95, 96, 97, 100, 101, 102, 103, 104, 107, 108,
109, 110, 115, 116-17, 121, 122, 126, 127, 128, 132, 133,
134, 135, 136, 137-41, 148, 149, 152, 153, 154, 156-57, 159,
161, 163, 165-66, 169, 173, 175, 176, 177, 179, 181, 182,
183, 186, 187, 189
imagination, 34, 37, 46-48, 83, 90, 134, 169-70, 172, 176, 180, 187;
    disavowed, 46; distinguished from desire, 187
    See also: slide projector, the
incest, 31, 44-45, 56, 156-58, 159-62, 165-69
In-Sink-Erator, the, 152
    See also: mind, the
insomnia, 6, 10, 21, 32, 53, 76, 145, 165, 174, 183
Ivory Coast, the, 34

James, Henry, 90; paraphrased, 22; quoted, 162, 183
James, William, paraphrased, 33
Jane Eyre (Brontë), 67, 68
Jimmy Jingle, 98
Judaism, 114, 116, 118; unique relation to literature, 116
Justine, daughter to Mercy and Hallamore, 31

Kant, Immanuel, 116-17, 160; paraphrased, 117
Kaufman, Eleanor, 186-87
Kazin, Alfred, 118
Kenny's Market, 76-77
King, Martin Luther, quoted, 6; assassinated by poets, 19
kitchen, the, 11, 13, 22, 73, 81, 89, 91, 92, 94, 96, 135, 145, 146,
    151, 177, 179, 180, 186, 187
kitchen sink, the, 11, 81, 90, 145, 146, 151-52, 174
Kunin, Aaron, confused with William, 29, 118
    See also: Kunin, William
Kunin, Natasha, gives reliable advice, 135; infatuation with Willy,
    167-68; reads boring novel, 5-6, 10, 20, 56; revises novel,
    64-65; sleeps, 5-165; speaks, 122, 143-44, 165-69, 171, 180
Kunin, William, bites Mercy, 9; brother to household objects,

147-48, 155; claims to have read *Waverly,* 150; compared
to dog, 169; confused with Aaron, 29, 118; confused
with Hallamore, 32-41; crushes centipede, 86-89; delivers
food to biology teacher, 5, 34; disturbed by open
cabinets, 174, 179; inability to talk, 24-28, 148-49;
infatuation with Hallamore, 37-40, 45, 89; infatuation
with Mercy, 46-48, 131-36; infatuation with surgeon, 171-
72, 187; kicked out of Natasha's house, 9-10, 157; molests
Natasha, 56, 159-62, 165-66; opens door, 147, 165; poor
vision of, 46-47, 169-70, 178-79, 185; reading block,
58-60, 82, 83, 84, 172, 178-79, 182, 184-85, 186-87;
rejected by Hallamore, 37-38; rejected by Mercy, 46-47,
131-35; "walking mind-body problem," 50; writes boring
novels, 6, 7, 10, 20, 22, 23, 40-41, 52, 56-65, 91, 114, 116,
157, 169
See also: Flavio; Justine; Kunin, Aaron

lakes, 11, 34, 64, 138, 184, 188
lamb roti, the, 51
Lang, Fritz, 85
Lapp, Sarah Jane, 137
laughter, 12, 38, 44-45, 67, 122-23, 127, 135, 168; and possession,
123, 125, 135
Lawrence, D.H., 185, 187
Lehr, Wendy, 34
letters, 7, 40-41, 97, 120, 128-29, 130, 177-78, 179, 180, 182, 185;
inscrutable, 128-29; unwritten, 171, 185
Letterman, David, 183
Levinas, Emmanuel, associated with deplorable tendencies in the
novel, 177
liberal arts, the, inadequate body of knowledge, 18-19
See also: art
library, the, 62-63, 182, 184
Lish, Gordon, 114
literature, 8, 17, 106, 114-19, 124-25, 139, 150, 156, 162; death of
serious l., 139; distinguished from surgery, 162; immunity

to, 115, 117; only Erin McGonagle produces, 118; outcast from, 114-18; problem of talking about, 119; speaks, 124, 125

Liu, Eric, 20

living room, the, 100, 105

love, 8, 13, 28, 44, 47, 62, 65, 76-77, 78, 100, 112, 118, 124, 145, 146, 150, 157; as illness, 157; for newspaper, 76-77; for pastry, 21-22, 56; for restaurant, 46-51

Lucifer, 153, 155

lying, 13, 40-41, 63, 124-25, 178, 185

McGonagle, Erin, arts administrator, 114-116; producer of literature, 118

Malaysia, 34

mandarin, the, 120

mangoes, 157

Maso, Carole, *Dunciad* attributed to, 129

masturbation, 42, 76, 100-104, 155; giving up m., 100, 104, 155; m. with newspaper, 76; m. with umbrella, 42

See also: tea

mathematicians, 18

Mattison, Alice, permission requested for "Fed-Exing the Bread," 64

menu, the, 24, 50, 51, 56, 61, 62, 142

meringues, 22, 56

Metropolis (Lang), 85

Miami, 50

Mies van der Rohe, Ludwig, 7

milkshake, the, 21-22

mind, the, 23, 27, 28, 29, 37-40, 46, 50, 65, 85, 90, 91-92, 104, 107-108, 122, 126, 135, 138, 143, 147, 152, 165, 167, 171, 172, 187; compared to In-Sink-Erator, 152

mind-reading, 57, 68, 82, 90, 173

Minneapolis, 9-10, 13, 16-19, 40, 42, 45, 46-47, 57, 66, 81, 98, 102, 106-108, 114, 116-17, 130, 152, 155, 156, 170, 171-72, 188; immunity to literature, 117; lacustrine city, 40; return

salt, 23, 159-60, 162

Santa Claus, 7

saucepan, the, 92, 165

Savran's (bookstore), 120, 184

Schoenberg, Arnold, 184; and modernism, 183

Scholes, Robert, 185-87; collapses on Willy, 186; lectures on
      Wagner, 187

Scott, Walter, 150

sculpture, 139, 173, 174

serene envelope, the
      See: sleep; newspaper, the

Sesame and Lilies (Ruskin), 106, 138

sex
      See: incest; masturbation; rape

Shakespeare, William, 6, 16, 19; quoted, 6

shame, 24-27, 105, 108-13, 123, 155; material for art, 105

shame-artist, the, 105-13; struck by can, 112-13; identified as Saul
      Bellow, 112
      See also: Bellow, Saul; Carbonell, Mercy

shit, 5, 7, 9, 19, 28, 29, 45, 58, 96, 98, 116, 146

sidewalk, the, 6, 9, 10, 16-18, 71, 75, 188; complains, 16-18; resents
      hopscotch, 17

Siegfried (Wagner), 187

Singapore, 34

sky, the, 9, 13, 16-18; described, 130; resents astronomy, 18;
      complains, 16-18

sleep, 5, 6, 7, 9, 10, 19, 20, 27, 29, 32-33, 34, 37, 38, 42, 43, 48-50,
      53, 56, 58, 65, 71, 72, 76, 80-81, 89, 91-92, 101, 105, 122,
      124, 137, 143-44, 146, 156, 159-60, 163-64, 165, 167-68,
      169, 174, 176, 180, 181, 184, 187; as envelope, 72-73, 163-
      64; desire for s., 53, 146, 168, 187

slide projector, emblem of imagination, 46-48, 168, 169; turned
      off, 46; turned on, 50
      See also: images; imagination

snow, 6, 9, 11, 13, 76-77, 120, 130, 156, 172; newspaper buried in,
      76-77; paper blows across, 130; shoveling, 6; suitcase

FENCE BOOKS

The Motherwell Prize

Unspoiled Air   Kaisa Ullsvik Miller

The Alberta Prize

The Cow   Ariana Reines
Practice, Restraint   Laura Sims
A Magic Book   Sasha Steensen
Sky Girl   Rosemary Griggs
The Real Moon of Poetry and Other Poems   Tina Brown Celona
Zirconia   Chelsey Minnis

Fence Modern Poets Series

Star in the Eye   James Shea
Structure of the Embryonic Rat Brain   Christopher Janke
The Stupefying Flashbulbs   Daniel Brenner
Povel   Geraldine Kim
The Opening Question   Prageeta Sharma
Apprehend   Elizabeth Robinson
The Red Bird   Joyelle McSweeney

Anthologies & Critical Works

Not for Mothers Only: Contemporary Poets on Child-Getting & Child-Rearing
Catherine Wagner & Rebecca Wolff, editors

Free Choice Poetry

Rogue Hemlocks	Carl Martin
19 Names for Our Band	Jibade Khalil Huffman
Bad Bad	Chelsey Minnis
Snip Snip!	Tina Brown Celona
Yes, Master	Michael Earl Craig
Swallows	Martin Corless-Smith
Folding Ruler Star	Aaron Kunin
The Commandrine and Other Poems	Joyelle McSweeney
Macular Hole	Catherine Wagner
Nota	Martin Corless-Smith
Father of Noise	Anthony McCann
Can You Relax in My House	Michael Earl Craig
Miss America	Catherine Wagner

Free Choice Fiction

The Mandarin	Aaron Kunin
Flet: A Novel	Joyelle McSweeney